Paddy Joe

Joyce Stranger

A CAROUSEL BOOK
TRANSWORLD PUBLISHERS LTD.

PADDY JOE

A CAROUSEL BOOK 0 552 522 34 1

First published in Great Britain by Collins Ltd.

PRINTING HISTORY

Collins edition published 1971
Carousel edition published 1983

Carousel Books are published by
Transworld Publishers Ltd.,
Century House, 61–63 Uxbridge Road,
Ealing, W.5.

To Norman H. Evans and the children of Queen's Road Primary School

Chapter One

The sun flared briefly, and died in a riot of colour. Night leaped over the horizon, devouring day.

Paddy Joe shifted his position. He had been perched in the fork of the old apple tree for so long that he had pins and needles in his left hand. His right foot was cramped, and he was drowning in darkness. Below him his three-year-old Alsatian dog, Storm, lay sphinx-like, only the twitch of an ear, flicking off a fly, revealing that he was alive. Paddy Joe reached down a bare foot and scratched the dog's back. Storm turned his head and thoughtfully licked the boy's ankle. Companionship restored, Paddy Joe changed his position, and resumed his thoughts.

The night was welcome. The soft murmur of the wind rustling through dry leaves soothed Paddy Joe. He had lived through a week of terror, and it was not yet over. He had come to the tree for sanctuary. The house was no longer friendly. Here he could be alone, and here he could think.

It was peaceful, sitting outside in the night. He was part of the shadows, fitting into darkness, being, and not feeling. He knew the rough bark was harsh against his hand. He was aware of the wind, blowing against his right cheek. It was the first time for a whole week that he had been at peace. It was also the last time, for tomorrow all this must end.

Tomorrow, they told him, he must leave the overgrown shrubby garden, where every plant was familiar, from the thicket where he often hid with Storm to the little wooden hut where his grandmother sat and wrote letters, gracing it by the name of summer house, though it was barely more than a shed. Grandee would never write letters again. Paddy Joe had not allowed himself to think of that before, lest the thought overwhelmed him and he betrayed himself when there were strangers about. Now only the darkness watched him, and he did not care.

He leaned back against the tree, and stared up at a sky splintered by faint stars, hanging flinty-sharp and remote, far away, suspended in nothingness. He concentrated on the stars, not wanting to examine the thoughts that, he knew, he must examine. Grandee had always said you must not push unpleasantness away. Take it out and look at it hard, and often it would shrink and vanish. This unpleasantness was not likely to shrink. It was more likely to grow. Meanwhile, for the moment, he would cease to be Patrick Joseph Rafferty, whom everybody called Paddy Joe, and he would be part of the night, an animal in its lair, waiting and watching, and reading the wind.

He wondered what Storm could smell, down there in the long grass, almost hidden from sight. Paddy Joe could smell little green apples, sour as disappointment. He could smell the old donkey beyond the hedge, a warm comforting smell, reminding him of rides on old Moke's back, and summer picnics, and swimming in the little river that shivered in the shallows beyond the garden wall.

He could smell wild flowers and grass and a fox that was loping by. His foot, resting on Storm's back, felt the tremor of excitement that seized the dog, and he hushed him quickly, not wanting to be seen, or heard. Martha thought he was in his room. She would worry and fuss if she knew he was out in the garden in the dark.

An owl cried its loneliness, whispering past on loose

feathered wings. It whooped again and was swallowed by the trees. A faraway diesel train yowled twice as it entered a distant tunnel. Its wheels approached, almost uncanny, a noise that grew in the night, and then, beyond the wall, Paddy Joe saw the lighted windows and the heads of people who were safe and protected, and who did not know that he sat in the lonely garden, facing a future that was dark as an abyss and much more frightening. He wished he could fall into safety again, but safety was gone. The world was peopled by strangers, and he belonged nowhere.

Now he had to face the thoughts that terrified him. Grandee was dead. He had lived with her since his parents died in an aircrash when he was only one year old. He had been staying with her and with Martha, who had been a sort of nurse to his mother. She had come back as a sort of nurse to him, and had stayed on, to help Grandee, who felt she was rather old to bring up a small boy on her own. Grandee had done her very best, even to ensuring that there were men in his life, and her friend, Colonel Brown, who lived on the other side of the rise, beyond her garden, had taught Paddy Joe to ride, and to shoot with a small bore rifle, and had also taught him to swim.

The Colonel's servant, who had once been his batman, Tomkin, had taught Paddy Joe too. He had taught him some surprising things, so that Paddy Joe knew how to live like a commando; how to creep, unseen, up to an enemy, and jump him; knew how to take advantage of the wind when they were stalking a deer to photograph as it grazed in the woods; and how to fish from the willow pool, and make a fly so real that trout found it tastier than the flies that danced on the shimmer above the water.

Grandee had been father and mother. She had been home, and rough comfort when he fought at school. She had no time for cosseted boys.

"One day, you'll be on your own, Paddy Joe," she had said, "I want to be sure you can cope. Life's not easy and it's not fair either, and don't you forget it. All you can do is make the best of whatever happens. No-one can escape the bad times."

There had been bad times. But nothing as bad as this. This, had begun a week ago, on the last day of school, just before the long summer holidays. Colonel Brown and Tomkin had gone away to Scotland, as they always did, from the middle of July until the middle of August. One year, they promised, Paddy Joe could go with them, but not this year. He and Grandee and Martha were going to a hotel on the South Coast, where there was a riding school that would improve his riding. He was going to learn to jump, and in the afternoons he and Storm could wander on the windswept beaches, and swim in the surf, and life would be an endless pleasure, to be savoured intensely. He had been looking forward with excitement to breaking-up day and the beginning of his long freedom.

They had come for him at the end of the second lesson, when he had been struggling with geometry, thinking that this was the last time for weeks that he would be shut in a stuffy classroom while the sun was shining on the river and the trout were rising under the willow. That night he would slip out and see if he could see the otters playing in the willow pool, as he need not get up early in the morning.

They told him that Grandee was dead. She had stepped off the kerb as a car came round the corner. The driver had no chance. She knew nothing, no pain, no time for fright or sorrow. She had gone. Paddy Joe stared at them. It was too difficult to believe. He could not believe it when the funeral was over and the people who knew him spoke to him awkwardly, not knowing what to say. He could not believe it, now, though Martha never stopped crying. Her nose was bright red and her eyes were shiny and whenever she saw him she said,

"Oh, Lambie, Lambie, what's to become of us all?"

Paddy Joe could not imagine. Martha was too old to look after him alone. For the last few months Grandee had had to do everything, as Martha's legs were slowly becoming so painful that she could walk only a few steps and her arms were so frail she could not carry the trays. Paddy Joe was worried about Martha, but he was more worried about himself. He had not a single relation in the world. If only he knew where Brownie had gone, but the colonel left no address. He was in the remote Highlands, where, for four weeks each year he fished with total singlemindedness, not writing a letter, or leaving an address at which he could be reached. It was his escape time. If he had been here Paddy Joe could have gone and talked to him, and to Tomkin. He could have worried out his position in life as Storm worried at the old shoe that was his to chew whenever he needed to chew. But the colonel was not there.

Everyone seemed to be going on holiday. People had come to see him, but had not known what to do, and had gone about their own affairs. Mr Throstle, Grandee's lawyer, had told him he would have to go away, as he could not stay alone with Martha, who herself needed to be looked after now. Mr Throstle had not told him where. He would know in the morning. Tomorrow he would go to strangers, he and Storm.

Tonight he was saying goodbye to the apple tree, as aware of the flavour of darkness as a fox in his den, savouring the last few hours of familiarity. It was too hot to sleep, and he could not bear the thought of his bed. He was bathed in the scent of the garden, of the big bush of soft pinky-lilac moss-roses, and the delicate sharp smell of the honeysuckle that rambled over the summer house. The stone house which had been his home for so long was a dark bulk, crouched among the trees that sheltered it.

Without Grandee to liven it, without her tall figure and stern face that softened to beauty when she smiled, the house was empty and soulless. The rooms were bleak and desolate in spite of the fires that old Martha lighted to try to give warmth to the loneliness. She was going away too, in the morning. Paddy Joe had to escape her. He could not comfort her and he could not bear seeing her grief. It made his own misery intolerable.

The window beside the apple tree flashed into light. Storm lifted his head and his eyes glowed. Paddy Joe flattened himself against the tree, not wanting to be seen. His foot warned the dog, and Storm froze obediently. It was a signal that he knew well. Paddy Joe used it frequently.

The lower pane of the big sash window was pushed high. Paddy Joe looked at the two men who entered the room. He realised that he had heard their cars, but had not taken in the fact that they had arrived. The first to come into his view was the vicar, a tall man whose bald head emphasised an anxious expression that never seemed to lighten. He was frowning now, his eyes on his companion.

The second man was Mr Throstle, Grandee's lawyer. He was a small man with a bent back and a head too big for his body. His sharp nose was inquisitive as a terrier's, and the only other thing noticeable about him was his tremendous feet, on which he always wore very shiny polished black shoes that dominated everything about them.

"Does the boy know?" the vicar asked.

"Time enough in the morning." The lawyer's voice

was as harsh as a crow at the dawn chorus. "They are coming to pick him up at ten. You can tell old Martha. Her wits were never bright, but now they're fairly addled. Fairly addled!"

He had a maddening way of repeating everything he said.

"Paddy Joe won't take it kindly," the vicar said thoughtfully. He was staring into the fire, and his white hands twisted together, over and under, skin whispering against skin with an unrecognisable noise that caused Storm to cock his head, listening. Paddy Joe did not hear it, and wondered what could be interesting the dog.

"Patrick has to learn. His grandmother spoilt him." The voice was harsher than ever. "Ridiculous, an old woman like her bringing up a boy. Even her name was eccentric. Grandee, indeed."

"The colonel named her." The vicar had moved into the centre of the room, and his expression was even more anxious. It suddenly dawned on Paddy Joe that the two men were quarrelling, without heat, without show, but with deadly animosity that tainted the atmosphere of the room so that he could feel it.

"Colonel Brown always called her Grande Dame, in fun. The boy abbreviated it to Grande D; hence Grandee. I see no harm in it." The vicar looked about him uneasily. Paddy Joe, who had never thought about this before, realised that the vicar did not like Mr Throstle either.

"Another eccentric. Two old people trying to bring up a boy. The whole thing was ridiculous. He should have been sent away to school. I told her. I told her repeatedly." The lawyer's face was flushed and his sharp nose twitched suddenly, rabbit-like. "My clerk will take the boy in the morning."

"And the old lady?" the vicar asked.

13

"I've arranged for her to go to a place where she'll be looked after. The matron is a good soul, and Martha will have a nice room and a companion to share it. She'll be very happy, very happy." The croaking voice was maddening Paddy Joe. He had a sudden urge to pull one of the sharp green apples and hurl it at the nose. He gripped his hands round his knee. Something moved at the edge of the light. A head poked into the fan of brightness and Paddy Joe relaxed. It was only his tortoise, obeying an urge to wander by moonlight. He concentrated on the horny back, willing the men to go away and leave him with the pack of new thoughts that chased through his head like hounds out of control. He needed to marshal them and order them. He had missed some of the conversation, but a sentence from the vicar startled him into attention again.

"What about the dog?"

Paddy Joe's heart began to misbehave. It bumped against his ribs and for a moment seemed to have slipped up into his throat, where it was choking him. Grandee had bought Storm for him three years ago. The two of them were inseparable. On schooldays Storm came to the bus-stop with him and watched him go. At teatime the dog was always waiting, lying beside the hedge. The drivers had grown so used to him that they hooted when Paddy Joe was aboard and everyone on the bus grinned as the dog, hearing the horn, leaped up, tail beating in wild excitement that exploded into joy as Paddy Joe jumped off the bus. The two greeted one another as if they had been apart for years instead of a few brief hours of the day.

"The old lady should never have bought the dog," the harsh voice was saying. "I warned her. A most unsuitable breed and a bad history. A starved pup that had been ill-treated and beaten and taken away from its owner in the first place. Heaven knows what vice lies

14

hidden. Heaven alone knows."

Paddy Joe had never been so angry in his life. Anger made him shake, made him want to thump his fists and scream, and was so apparent that Storm growled softly and Paddy Joe had to silence him fast with his foot pressed into the dog's shoulder, asking for instant obedience. Storm lay quiet, but his body throbbed with tension. The boy was aware of leashed muscles, ready to spring.

"The vet will put the dog down as soon as my clerk has taken the boy to St Martin's," the harsh voice said. "It's all for the best."

"I don't like it," the vicar said.

"Have you any other suggestion? Answer me that. Answer me that."

The light went out and the room was dark and the voices died. Paddy Joe thought that he would die too. He had not imagined that anything worse could happen than Grandee's death. Now he knew he was wrong, and he curled up at the foot of the apple tree with his face buried in Storm's fur, unable to face the future at all, or take out any of his worries and look at them, as he knew they could not shrink. They would grow enormous, and blot out the past, until it was a hidden memory, so treasured that it could never be shared or spoken about.

Two cars drove away. Paddy Joe no longer had a body. He did not know that he was dashing his hand against the rough bark, or that blood was trickling down his wrist. He could feel nothing. He could see nothing. His inside was one enormous knotted pain. His mouth and throat ached with misery and his eyes burned. He thought of being shut away in St Martin's, a children's home in the heart of a town, away from trees and the silent woods, with boys crowding him on every side; with no privacy, no time to be alone and watch and think. Never again to see the magpies parade on the rockery or the crows wrench at the twiggy trees to break off sticks for their nests, or the squirrels bury their nuts. It was unthinkable.

Never to feel Storm's warm body against him again. He put out a hand to reassure himself that the dog was there, was breathing and alive and close against him. He buried his nose in the fur of the Alsatian's ruff, smelling the comfortable dog smell that was as familiar to Paddy Joe as breathing. Grandee had taken the terrified ill-treated pup, when she heard about him, and had trained him, with Tomkin's help, into a brilliantly obedient dog. Paddy Joe did the rest himself, learning to know his animal, and he and Storm were not boy and dog, but partners, one helping the other. Storm's nose told Paddy Joe of things that he would never have seen, like the kingfishers' nest in the hole in the bank under the willow tree, and the traces left by the otters after their fishing. Tomkin had shown Paddy Joe how to interpret his dog's language and now the two of them had a sympathy that was almost uncanny to those who knew nothing about dogs.

Paddy Joe could not stop remembering. Storm had been small and frightened, a shivering unhappy tormented little creature, and Grandee had taught him trust. He had loved and obeyed the old lady, but he soon learned that he belonged, every hair of his fur, every whisker of his face, every heartbeat of his body, to Paddy Joe.

When work was done they walked together in the woods, or went with Tomkin to track roe deer, and look for the marks of the bucks that brooded in summer cover, the does that walked daintily down the forest ride, and the tiny tell-tale track of the hooves of the kids. Often they saw a family party, and hid, until the wind betrayed them and the deer vanished as if they had never been, melting into shadows that were secret as night.

Together he and Storm explored the fields and swam in the river, diving into the pool beneath the old willow whose roots sheltered the otter and her cubs. Together they traced the line taken by the fox, or chased after rabbits, free to come and to go as the hare herself as she fled along the furrow. Paddy Joe was a solitary child. He lived at the end of a long lane, five miles from school and from the town which sheltered the children's home that he was to be sent to in the morning. He found companionship in the dog, and pleasure in the woods, and solace by the river.

If only Brownie were here. He would not let such a terrible thing happen. Brownie would take Storm. You couldn't put such a young dog to sleep. It wasn't fair. And out of the darkness came the memory of Grandee's quiet voice saying "Life's not fair. Remember that when the bad times come. Sometimes you'll feel that the good times aren't fair either. But you can't avoid the bad times. None of us can."

Paddy Joe sat up and wiped his hand across his eyes. He had to think. He had to plan. He was alone in the world and no one at all cared what happened to him. He only had his dog. He knew, with total clarity, what he must do. He and Storm must run away. All he needed was to keep the dog alive until the colonel came home. Just two weeks – fourteen more days. Such a short time – and such a long time. Brownie and Tomkin would think of something together. Grandee said difficulties were created in order to be faced. Paddy Joe would face up to this one by himself. He stood up and brushed the grass off his clothes. He had a lot of planning to do.

A voice called in the darkness.

"Paddy Joe!"

Chapter Two

Martha was calling. It was late and he should have been in bed long ago. The garden was silent. The wind had faltered to a sleepy murmur, and nothing stirred. Paddy Joe walked towards the house, a tall boy whose dark hair fell into an elflock over one brown eye, and was forever pushed impatiently back with slender sun-tanned hands. He shook the long strands back now, and flicked his fingers to Storm, and went inside the house as the church clock tolled the hour and the owl cried to the moon and the wind suddenly stirred itself so that the restless trees swayed against the night, and the river sobbed with its own noise as it fled to the faraway sea.

The kitchen was too warm after the freshness of the garden. Martha bustled about, losing her misery in busyness. Her apron was dirty, tied loosely round her thin middle, and her grey hair straggled from its bun, giving her an unfamiliar untidiness. Her eyes were red and bright, but she managed the trace of a smile.

"I made you something special," she said. "You didn't have no tea."

It was far too late for tea. He had forgotten the need to eat. Everything had been topple turvy since Grandee died. Nothing looked right. The kitchen clock had stopped, as time had ceased to matter. The fire burned sulkily in a welter of ash and there was dust on the Windsor chairs. But the table was laid for two, and Martha had cooked his favourite meal of egg and chips and she had made pancakes and a blueberry pie, and there was cream. Paddy Joe thought he would never be hungry again, but he made himself eat, and the food put some comfort back into his body. Martha ate too, playing with the food, trying desperately to make some kind of conversation. Paddy Joe tried to talk back, but was aware of nothing but the fact that he was suddenly burning hot, and his face was uncomfortably flushed.

Conversation faltered and stopped. It was too difficult. Martha could only think that in the morning she had to go away, had to be shut in a home for old people among other old people, and tomorrow they would have to tell the boy that he could not take his dog, and that the dog must be put down. It choked her to think of it, and to see Storm, who had gobbled his supper and was now busy gnawing a huge bone which she had made a special effort to bring for him. He was stretched on the hearth-rug by the fire, where he had no right. Paddy Joe found it difficult to concentrate on eating, without trying to talk as well, or to tell the dog to move to his proper place. He finished his food, and helped Martha clear away and wash up without being asked, and that alone was almost enough to make the old woman cry again, but she managed to restrain herself, and wished that the evening might go on for ever and tomorrow never come.

Paddy Joe watched Martha wind the clock and set it right. It was very late. Long past bed-time, and almost tomorrow now. It was an unpleasant and frightening thought. So little of the night was left. Paddy Joe went to the stairs and whistled his dog. Storm stared, surprised. The bedrooms were out of bounds, but Martha did not check him. It was the dog's last night, and let the boy have him. Tears flooded down the soft pouchy cheeks and she turned hastily away as Storm raced upstairs, delighted to spend the night with his master.

Tomorrow——

Paddy Joe stared out of his bedroom window. The

moon shone on the willow and wind rippled the water. He thought suddenly of the book he had been reading, he and Grandee. They took it in turns in the evening to read to one another, cosy beside the fire, the light shining on his grandmother's silky white hair, friendliness flooding the room. They had been reading *The Lord of the Rings*, and were almost halfway through, both of them mesmerised by the rhythm of the words. The river beyond the garden was just like the river in the book, the Brandywine, along which the hobbits had made their mysterious journey. They too had left home to avoid unknown and terrible dangers, and perhaps death. They had met all kinds of adventures.

The owl cried again. Its voice was a challenge. Paddy Joe knew what he had to do.

He would put off tomorrow for ever. Thinking about the book had helped to clarify his ideas. He would leave home and avoid death for Storm and imprisonment for himself. He would feel like an animal in a cage at the Zoo, shut up in the town. He had always been free to wander wherever he chose so long as Storm was with him, and often he slipped out at night and joined Tomkin on some expedition, to watch badger cubs roll and play or the vixen teach her young. He had seen otters slide down the river bank, and seen the owl wing home with a mouse in her mouth, to feed her sheltering nestlings. He could not be shut in a city, made to obey rules by day and by night. He and Storm would follow the river as the hobbits had followed the Brandywine. Perhaps there really was a riverdaughter and elffolk who might help him. If only he too had a ring of invisibility.

He sighed, and returned to reality. He drew the curtains close so that no chink of light would shine into the darkness. By morning he and Storm must be as far away as possible. He had to make his plans very carefully so that nothing could go wrong.

Paddy Joe looked about him, wondering if he would ever see this room again. He had grown up here, lived here for almost the whole of his life, and there was a lifetime packed into it. He would never sleep in the bunk bed against the wall again, or stand on the coloured prayer mat that the colonel had given him, or handle the slender rod that Tomkin had made for his last birthday, a rod so light and beautifully balanced that it was impossible not to catch fish with it.

He would never see the pictures on the walls again: the big picture of the stallion thundering across the prairie, that faced the sketch of the slender mare, dipping her head to graze, the wind fingering her mane. On the opposite wall were his pin-ups, pictures cut from magazines, and postcards sent by his friends, all kept for a special reason, all dear and familiar. Everything, Martha said, would have to be sold, but these, surely, were his.

Some he could not bear to leave. They would take up so little room. He began to tear them from the wall. The badger, scenting the air, as she left her sett, her cubs behind her, came first. Tomkin had sent him that one from Scotland the year before. There was a postmark on it, and Paddy Joe turned it over with quick hope, but the mark was smudged and totally unreadable. Beside it was the card the colonel sent the same year, also with a smudged postmark. An owl with wings outspread feathered across a dark sky, staring straight into the camera lens. Paddy Joe looked at the postmark until his eyes ached, trying to decipher the name, but it was useless. It might have been Invernay or Inverness, Inverary, or Invertarn. It might be anywhere. He gave up and began to pack again. There were others treasured from long ago; one of two mountain ponies, grazing together; another of two foxes, standing in the snow, while beside them a squirrel stood on hindlegs eating a nut; and beyond them an Arab stallion gazed across the desert, and another card bore on it the pictures of six different types of mouse, and their Latin names. One day, he had intended to make a scrap book, but there had never been time.

Now there was no more time, but the cards would bring the thoughts of home to him, no matter where he went. There were so many memories hidden in them; memories of school friends and of friends of Grandee, who had known his passion for animals; memories of Tomkin and the colonel, and times spent in their company. Paddy Joe thought back to the last day before their holidays. He and Tomkin had been fishing. Shadows lay across the river bank, and a small deer came down to drink. It dipped its head, perfection mirrored in a smooth surface that was suddenly fractured by the drinking muzzle. Tomkin gently raised one hand, thumb upward, and Paddy Joe had nodded. They did not need words to communicate. The sight brought rapture to both of them. Storm, stretched at his master's feet, froze obediently when told, but remained eager, tense, ears cocked, body ready to run, and sighed deeply when the deer melted into the darker part of the copse, and he was not released to chase.

Paddy Joe looked across the room at the puzzled Alsatian, who was watching every move. If only he could talk to the dog, could make him understand, could make him help, but he remained a dog, and was perhaps all the more valued for that. Storm needed Paddy Joe, who had helped him forget the misery of his puppyhood, and Paddy Joe, more than ever before in his life, needed Storm. That anyone should take him from him was unthinkable.

Paddy Joe could not bear the thought. He looked about him, planning busily. The cards were ready to

23

pack and the wall was bare, as if he had already taken leave of the room, stripping it for a new occupant. He wondered who would come and live here now. Strangers would change the garden, and neaten its secret places. Strangers would walk in the familiar rooms, bringing their own furniture and belongings, and none of them would know that here, once, lived Paddy Joe. They would never guess the hours he had spent in this room; hours of happiness, building stories around the animals on his post cards, listening to his own records on the record player that Grandee had given him two years ago. He would miss that too. He wished he could play one of his favourites for the last time, but that would rouse Martha. In any case he had no time.

There was a great deal to do.

Work, Paddy Joe discovered, was a good way of forgetting worries. He took paper and pencil, and the dog watched him, mystified by such activity in the night when people usually slept. They needed clothes and food, and a way of avoiding capture. Who, Paddy Joe wondered, would be likely to look for them? His heart began to thump again as he realised that very likely Mr Throstle, finding him gone, would send for the police. And the police would bring dogs on his trail. He would need all the craft that Tomkin ever taught him.

Paddy Joe changed his clothes. He put on jeans and a clean shirt and found a thick jersey which he stored in his rucksack; a change of thick socks and his good scouting shoes, which had taken him for miles on hikes. He added his scout beret, as it might seem more natural to see a scout with a rucksack than an ordinary boy. He dared not take his uniform as that had the troop's number on it and would make him easy to identify.

He found the dented old cash box which had

belonged to his father, kept in a secret place at the back of his cupboard. It was one of his most treasured possessions, but it was too unwieldy to pack. He would have to leave it behind. There were 63p in the box. That would not go far. He dared not slip down to the kitchen to find food, lest Martha heard him, as she only slept in catnaps, dozing and waking, often wandering about the house at night to make herself a cup of tea. She might wander tonight. Paddy Joe took his winter coat and laid it along the door to hide the crack of light. He did not want any interruption.

He needed his sleeping bag, and a big polythene sheet, that would cover him in rain, and keep wet from his sleeping bag, and keep Storm dry too. He had camped with the scouts, and knew what to pack. His sheath knife would be useful, and his plastic mug. His penknife, which had a thick blade and a thin blade, and a spike for getting stones out of horse-shoes. His stamp tweezers, to get splinters out of his hands and thorns out of Storm's pads. A pair of scissors. A comb. His hair would soon be very long, and if it was very untidy it might call attention to himself. He packed a cake of soap, as a clean boy would attract less attention than a very dirty one. Tomkin had taught him that, exclaiming in horror whenever he saw a grubby urchin who looked as if he had no home at all. If he became dirty he would look much more lost than if he managed to stay neat. No-one must notice him.

String. That was always useful. There was a bar of chocolate in his desk. A warm anorak. He could not carry too much, but he needed to be warm and dry, as there was no one to look after him if he became ill now. Illness was something he dared not risk. A new worry flared in his mind. Suppose Storm caught a germ and needed a vet? There was no money to pay for that either. Perhaps he could earn some, only how did you set about earning money when you were only twelve, even if you looked older? Time enough to think of that when they had started on their way.

Paddy Joe looked at the calendar. It was only just the start of August and Colonel Brown and Tomkin would not be home until August 15th. There was a long time to go. He did not know if he could last so long, but Tomkin had taught him well and he would have a very good try. Thinking of Tomkin made him think of fish. He dared not take his rod as that again would make him conspicuous but he had a handline and several hooks and two weights that Tomkin had given him for his last birthday, telling him he could fish off the pier at the seaside and catch a whale. It had been a great joke between them.

Paddy Joe packed carefully, putting the hooks in a small tin so that they did not catch in his clothes or his hands. A fish hook could give you a nasty time, as it went in deep and had to be cut out. He must watch Storm too, or the dog might tread on one of the spares and injure himself. There was a lot to remember.

It was almost three in the morning before Paddy Joe was satisfied. He had one last job. He took off the labels from all the clothes he was wearing, and the name tapes. From now on he was not Paddy Joe Rafferty. He was Pat Jones, and he was camping with his parents and his dog, and was temporarily lost. If he met anyone who asked questions, he was on his way to join them. The scout beret was put at the bottom of the pack for emergencies.

Storm could not wear his everyday collar as that had his name and address engraved on it. Paddy Joe had a choke chain, and he brought it out and slipped it round the dog's neck. Storm looked astounded, and then realised that, even though it was very late, this was one of their night-time escapades. His tail began to wag eagerly against the floor and once more Paddy Joe hushed him. He was thankful now that he had spent so much time training the dog.

Paddy Joe took one last look round the room. *The Lord of the Rings* lay on his bedside table. The book was thick and it was heavy, but it was comforting to have, and it might give him ideas if he met trouble. It had given him one idea already. It just fitted into the rucksack.

Paddy Joe turned out the light and drew the curtains. The roof of the outhouse was just below his window and he and Storm had often gone that way to meet Tomkin, not wishing to wake Grandee. They slipped out now, two shadows in the darkness, moving as softly as the wind moved over the whispering grasses, careful not to knock a foot or scrape against the tiles. The edge of the roof led by an easy jump to a platform that Paddy Joe had made on top of the waterbutt, and from there it was a simple matter to jump to the ground, landing on soft earth that prevented them hurting themselves but also betrayed their footsteps.

They landed safely and Paddy Joe raked the ground carefully with his fingers, obliterating all marks. He had planned the next step in careful detail. They kept a cow and a calf in the shelter in the yard and every day Daisy and Bonnie were released in the orchard and brought in at night. Paddy Joe led the way to the cattle shelter and whistled under his breath to Storm to follow him inside. The boy trod hard, round and round the shelter, soaking his shoes in muck, and ensured that Storm's paws were also plastered. When he was certain that all was well done, he tracked across the yard in the path that Daisy and Bonnie left, as they followed the same trail every day, and led the way through the gate into the orchard.

A police dog seeking them would fail to find any scent

but that of the cattle. Not even Storm would leave a trail. Paddy Joe began to feel light-hearted at the prospect of baffling anyone who might be on his track. He was suddenly glad that he was not a hobbit, with the Night Riders following him, and the safety of the world in his pocket.

He looked back at the house and felt an ache inside him, a desolation of loneliness and a longing for Grandee and the comfort of her presence. It was no use longing. He turned away resolutely and set his mind on the days ahead. He needed to take every care and put all regret behind him, but the lump in his throat remained, an unwelcome reminder, and he swallowed and blinked away a mist that unaccountably clouded his eyes.

The far gate of the orchard led to the river bank. The moon had slipped out of the sky, and darkness hid both boy and dog in its skirts, sheltering them with a promise of freedom. Paddy Joe soon grew used to the night. The trees were black bulks looming beyond the clearings and the sky behind them was not so dark as the solid trunks. It was eerie, walking alone when all the world was asleep, knowing that they would stay alone. Tomkin would not be waiting by the willow, his homely sun-tanned face wrinkled and creasing into a sudden grin as he fluted his soft tuneless whistle.

Storm paced sedately, keeping to heel. Paddy Joe eased his rucksack, and heard, with quick relief, the sliding murmur of the swiftly flowing water. A thin light showed up the edges of the night. Day was stalking them, greying the black, soon to destroy cover. A dim gleam revealed the river, and Paddy Joe knew that here was his best means of foiling his pursuers. He and Storm together paddled through the ripples and the two of them covered almost a mile along the edge of the shingly shallows before dawn light spilled through the trees and colour returned to the world.

Chapter Three

The early morning sun flung brilliance over a clouded sky, pointing with flame the clouds that billowed over the trees. The wakening birds called their pleasure at the day's renewal; croon of dove vied with song of thrush and call of blackbird and twitter of sparrow, echoing through the wood until all the world seemed alive with their din.

Apart from the birds, they were alone. No one else was awake. It was hard for Paddy Joe to accept that Tomkin would not be waiting, his rod over his shoulder, his plans for the day's fishing bursting from him almost as soon as he saw Paddy Joe. It was sad to remember that the colonel's two hunters were both away at a livery stable; that the house, only a short walk from the wood, was empty, blind-windowed, and shuttered. It was not a good thought. It made the loneliness worse. Always before, when Paddy Joe slipped out before day was fully upon him, it had been for a fishing expedition, or an early ride on the heath, before cars spoiled the solitude of the quiet lanes. Loneliness was so intense that Paddy Joe ached. Storm, sensitive as always to the boy's mood, butted Paddy Joe's knee, and thrust his cold nose against his master's hand. Paddy Joe buried his fingers in the thick ruff round the dog's neck, and found comfort.

He had never felt so alone in his life. There was nowhere to go, and no one to welcome him. It was a daunting thought that darkened the dawning day with sorrow. It was a thought to avoid. Paddy Joe pushed it resolutely away, and tried to think of less frightening things.

Thought was betrayal. He suddenly remembered his tortoise, Sam. He had completely forgotten about Sam. Sam was a Mediterranean tortoise that Tomkin, driving to London, had found mysteriously wandering along the hard shoulder of the M1. Tomkin decided that a tortoise on a motorway constituted an emergency, and drove on to the hard shoulder himself. A passing police car followed him to see what was amiss, and, shown the tortoise, the two policemen stared at it in disbelief.

"My Sam!" said one of them. "How in the world did he get there?"

So Tomkin named him Sam and gave him to Paddy Joe. Sam adored bananas. He ate dandelions and lettuce, if nothing better was available. He also ate strawberries, and made havoc among the growing and ripening fruit. He enjoyed apples, and accepted a sliver of pear, but bananas provoked his tortoise soul to rapture. Bananas were his passion. He came every day, at about five o'clock, for three thick slices of the delicious fruit, which Paddy Joe cupped in his hand. The strange, wrinkled little head dipped to feed, the tiny mouth was damp against the boy's palm, tickling as the tortoise ate.

When Sam had finished he blinked his bright eyes, and drew his head into his shell, and retreated into his private darkness, where no one else could intrude. If bananas were missing Sam's reproachful eyes were misery to remember. Paddy Joe felt his sense of desolation deepen. No one would bring Sam bananas now. And what would happen when winter came? Paddy Joe had always given the tortoise a cardboard box filled with straw in which to hibernate. Would Sam find a dry warm place of his own where he would be safe if Paddy Joe never came back to fetch him?

As these thoughts fled through his mind Paddy Joe recognised his main fear. Suppose the colonel would not look after Storm? The colonel was old. Not as old as Grandee, as he had not been retired very long, but he lived on a pension, and grumbled about the price everything cost him, and sometimes said sadly that if expenses continued to soar, the horses would have to go. Storm was an expensive dog to feed. His daily ration of meat had cost Grandee a fortune. Martha often said so. Suppose at the end of two weeks, Paddy Joe returned to find only anger. Anger because he had run away, anger because Storm cost too much to keep, and must still be put to sleep; anger because he had taken matters into his own hands and defied the adult world.

Paddy Joe stopped walking. He had been thinking so hard that he had not noticed that the path was winding away from the river, and back again, touching the waterside at infrequent intervals. The sigh and thrust and swirl of water was always in his ears. The sun stronger now, though not yet very warm, was filtering through the trees. A squirrel scampered across the path, and stopped to stare at him. It was very young, certainly only born that year, and its tail was a thin rat's tail out of which untidy long hairs sprouted, giving the tiny beast an unfinished look, like the baby sparrows when they have not grown their long tail feathers. It chattered suddenly at the dog and raced up a tree trunk, peering inquisitively through the leaves when it reached safety.

Paddy Joe sat down, his back against the tree, and tried to sort his thoughts. Suppose he went back, now, before anyone realised he had gone. Suppose he asked the vicar for help. The vicar obviously didn't like Mr Throstle any more than Grandee had. But the vicar, though kind, was ineffectual. He could not control

31

either the choirboys or the scouts, and he certainly would be quite unable to cope with the forceful solicitor. Even Grandee had found Mr Throstle a handful.

"He means well, Paddy Joe," she had said once. "I have to say that for him, in all fairness. He exhausts me, though, and today was a particularly exhausting session. It's that trying, exacting, legal mind. I don't think there's a scrap of ordinary human consideration in the man. He's just a document case, stuffed full of rules and precedents and regulations."

It was no use asking help from the vicar. Paddy Joe would have to go his own lonely way and trust to luck. If only he were a hobbit. Here, where the river ran softly, and the trees crowded close to the bank, was surely the haunt of the river daughter. It was better to think of her, with her fair hair and green robes, among the flowers, than to ponder his own frightening situation. There, where sun fingered the water, and the ripples dazzled with light beneath the dreaming willows, rustling in the early morning breeze, Tom Bombadil must surely lurk, listening to the noise made by the water, and singing songs that sounded like waves sighing in the shallows.

The grasses parted. An otter looked about him, saw nothing threatening, and slid into the stream, only his head showing. The wash behind him was a solid Vee of white water. Storm pricked up his ears, but Paddy Joe pressed the dog against the ground, and for a moment they were part of the wild life about them, not boy and dog at all, but woodland creatures themselves, accepted and ignored. A butterfly danced on the wind, bright wings fluttering. A Red Admiral. Paddy Joe watched it, and for a few minutes, let his busy brain rest. His head was beginning to ache with thinking.

There was an arrow of light, a cleaving of the air, a

shimmer of brightness, a flash in the water. The kingfisher shattered the dazzle on the stream and flew up again, a miracle of colour, iridescent in the sun. The silver fish, twisting and struggling in its beak, caught the light too, and pattern from the trees, as the leaves flickered in the wind, hid and revealed them alternately. Paddy Joe watched. The kingfisher was rainbow light and rainbow promise, promise of a future that was safe and assured, one day, perhaps soon. The murmur in the trees soothed him as it answered the murmur of the water. A world where a kingfisher glowed in green dimness under the willows could not be entirely bad. Storm stretched his neck and leaned his head on Paddy Joe's knee, jealously demanding attention. Paddy Joe stroked the dog, and for a moment, both were at peace and entirely content.

Far away, a distant voice shouted. Paddy Joe, startled, jumped to his feet. He had forgotten time. Time was his enemy. So were the speeding minutes marked by relentless clocks whose shrill alarm bells must already be waking a reluctant workaday world from sleep. The alarm clock would waken Martha, who would dress, and go to call him, and find him gone. A clock would awaken the vicar, calling him to Matins. A clock, surely a noisy, busy, fussy clock with a masterful tick, would arouse Mr Throstle, undoubtedly to shine his enormous black shoes until they reflected his face.

Paddy Joe knew now how the hunted fox felt. He too was a fox and behind him, all ready to follow his trail, were the questing hound packs. Should they find him, his fate would be a cage, a dormitory in a faraway house in a town, his only privacy the dark of night, and his bed. And for Storm, there would be death in the morning.

They had to go. They had to hurry. They had to be as far away as possible and there was no time for dalliance.

Only he was hungry, and so was Storm. Paddy Joe began to run, anxious to make up for lost time. He had not slept all night, and had been half dozing, half dreaming, as he sat under the tree trying to escape his thoughts.

There were shadows under the trees, where the long trunks threw their darkness over the sun-sparkled ground. The shadows moved, and suddenly they were watchers with shining eyes. As Paddy Joe approached them, they vanished. He knew they were not real, as the dog did not growl at them. Storm paced on happily, enjoying the walk and the scents of the wood, totally content because he was with Paddy Joe, and not waiting alone at home while the boy went off to school. The shadows were deeper. The watchers threatened Paddy Joe with capture. He walked, soft-footed, careful not to break stick or twig, his eyes hunting the thickets. He held Storm's lead tightly. He did not like the feel of the woods today. When he walked in them with Tomkin they were total enchantment. Alone, with no hope of human company, they were fearsome.

It was easy to remember old stories of travellers waylaid by human wile or by witchcraft. He could see the witchwoman, her eyes fierce, her long hair blowing in a malignant wind that she had conjured to defeat him. She flung danger after danger in his way. Deep pit, and water hole. Trap, and a wall of glass. Evil-minded poachers, out to destroy. Paddy Joe watched the darkness under the trees so anxiously that he tripped over a snaking bramble stem and fell headlong, knocking every breath from his body. He gasped in pain and Storm, anxious, licked the boy's face. For one horrible moment Paddy Joe thought that some malicious spirit had indeed cast a spell, and then he saw the bramble branch and sat up and took himself severely in hand. He must concentrate on other matters. The difficulty was, on what?

The path snaked beside the river again. An insect hovered above the shallows. A silver fish arched out of the water. A trout! Paddy Joe looked hard at the ripples. He could concentrate on fish. Tomkin had taught him to visualise the fish's world, so that he would know where to cast his fly, and not waste time flogging empty waters.

The river was swift and shallow, sliding over rocks that had been weathered to smoothness by the centuries. The banks were mud and grass, holed here and there by otter and water rat, cut into coves and bays and tiny creeks and inlets where the pools were deeper and the fish could hide.

A swallow darted across the water. A dipper, standing on a fallen branch that lay across the stream, preened his feathers. Silver drops fell from his beak and he dipped his head and splashed water over himself, enjoying his bath. He flew to a nearby bush with a chatter of anger as something rustled in the bushes.

Storm crouched and growled. Paddy Joe tightened his hold, motioning the dog to silence. Ears cocked, eyes wide and bright, mouth open, tongue lolling, the dog waited, and suddenly relaxed. A large hedgehog, quite unconscious of the panic his noise had caused, moved on astonishingly swift legs across the grass and ran on to a shingly patch where the bank was low, and lapped from the shallows. Storm lost interest. He had once, in his puppy days, hurt his nose badly as he tried to sniff one of the bristly spiny beasts. It was an episode he would never forget. He was not interested in hedgehogs.

Paddy Joe was so hungry that he felt quite sick. He must have been walking for hours. He had left home at half past three. Yet it was only just after six in the morning. He was probably five miles from home. The faraway voice that he had heard some time before must have been a herdsman calling the cattle in to milking on a nearby farm. It was lucky that Daisy had her calf to feed from her. There was no one to milk her now. He had not realised that they had so many responsibilities. Storm, and Sam the tortoise, and the cow and her calf. All of them dependent on Grandee and with a future as uncertain as Paddy Joe's.

The future terrified him all over again, making him want to hurry, to be as far away as possible before Martha woke and called Mr Throstle. The rucksack pulled at his shoulders. The path twisted away from the river again, among arched trees that once more filtered sunlight that, only a moment before had been full on his face. It was cooler under the trees. The morning was still, the wind almost gone. Dappled shadows lay on the grass, and one of them moved suddenly. A roe deer barked nearby. The shadows must have hidden one of her kids, but its quick scramble for cover had deceived his eyes. Storm stiffened to attention, longing to run free, to hunt along the enticing trails that lay all round him, so that the ground and the air were pungent with scent that merged and mingled and sharpened excitement.

Paddy Joe knew none of them, but was aware that every drift of breeze brought news to the Alsatian. News of fox and stoat and badger, of pheasant roosting above them, of a guinea fowl, strayed from a farmhouse, hidden under a bush. A fieldmouse, quivering with terror, lay under a huge dock leaf. Storm sniffed at it, but did not touch it. Another scent had attracted him, and as the fieldmouse ran, its heart thumping in panic, the dog scraped at the ground, and moved a cluster of dead leaves.

Five guineafowl eggs lay in the hollow. Paddy Joe knew them at once, because the farmer near him kept the birds too, and Grandee liked their eggs. Also, the eggs would travel well, as the shells were so hard that you almost needed a hammer to break them. They could be dropped without harm. Paddy Joe slipped them into his pocket. No one would miss them, and the birds, like hens, laid frequently. The eggs might be fertile, but they were quite cold and the bird was not incubating them. It was a useful find, and if the worst came to the worst and he could not cook them, he could always break them and eat them raw, and Storm was often given a raw egg in milk as part of his diet, and would probably eat these too. It was an omen, and Paddy Joe began to feel more cheerful although he still needed to eat and could not yet face raw eggs.

Storm walked sedately. He was Paddy Joe's guardian, and his eyes watched, and his ears listened, alert for danger. Nothing and no one should harm the boy while the dog was near. The path had come back to the water again. It was a secret turfy path, beaten out by the feet of many animals as they went about their private business; unknown to most people, who followed the wide trails among the trees, unaware that below them, only a moment away, was the cool secrecy of the little river, twisting and turning between its banks, giving shelter to water rats and otters. There were also coypu that had escaped from captivity and found a new wilderness in a strange land where they thrived and bred and burrowed in the bank. Paddy Joe saw signs of them, but never glimpsed the beasts themselves.

Paddy Joe was thirsty. He walked down to the water and stooped to it, drinking from cupped hands, while beside him Storm lapped noisily, splashing the bright drops everywhere. They must have food. Paddy Joe did not want to eat the eggs. He would carry them for emergencies and emergency was not yet. There was a long time to go, and he must be careful. He had so little money and feeding himself was not going to be easy.

37

Perhaps he might try fishing in the shallows, but he had no bait and no time to dig for worms. No decent trout fisherman would ever fish with worms, but fishermen were seldom so hungry that they had to rely on what they caught to keep them alive.

Paddy Joe looked carefully at the river. He had never come so far as this to fish. He tried to remember all that Tomkin had taught him. There, where the bank was steep, and an overhang jutted out above the stream, a big trout might shelter. It looked a good place for a fish to lie, and use as his home base, darting out to feed in his territory. Like every creature on land, every four-footed beast, every bird, every reptile, each fish had his own home, and his own hunting ground, that he defended fiercely against all enemies. On his own ground, he was king. If he strayed, he was an intruder, to be beaten off, and defeated, and, unless he was a very unusual creature, he would run, and leave the owner to his victory.

If there was a fish there, it could not see above the overhang. Trout were clever, and sharp-eyed, and a strangeness on their horizon, caused by man or animal, sent the fish into hiding, seeking safety. Anything unknown threatened danger. Paddy Joe lay quite flat, and cautioned Storm so that the dog lay quiet, completely still. The Alsatian knew about fishing, but not this kind of fishing, and watched, puzzled. Paddy Joe was interested in the river, which was not unusual, but he had no rod or line. Paddy Joe edged forwards, careful not to show himself. He stretched his arm towards the water, slowly, carefully, an inch at a time, feeling until he met the cold surface, and slipped his hand under, against the bank. There, sure enough, was a trout.

Paddy Joe breathed in, remembering what Tomkin had told him. His fingers slipped gently along the smooth body, tickling the underside, so that the fish felt nothing but ecstasy, a delight in the sensation that spread over his skin.

The exploring fingers moved on, until Paddy Joe reached the tell-tale gill-slits, and at once his hand slid inside, holding tightly. The fish arched and twisted, thrashing under the water, striving to get away from the crippling hold that had suddenly developed from nowhere. Paddy Joe lifted and pulled and the trout landed on the bank, its body flapping. The tail slapped down on Storm's paw, and he looked at the fish inquisitively and sniffed it.

"Kill fast, and kill mercifully."

Tomkin might have been there beside him, so plain were his often repeated instructions, sounding inside the boy's head. Paddy Joe found a smooth stone that fitted his hand. One hard blow stopped the struggling fish, and for a moment, looking at the patterned body, lying still on the sunny bank, Paddy Joe felt sadness and guilt. But he had killed to eat, and even Lord Baden Powell himself had allowed that. The trout was a good size, almost, he thought, a pound and a half in weight. It would provide breakfast. He felt like a poacher and a thief until he remembered that the fishing licence that the colonel had given him for his birthday covered all the river. Even if he had not caught the trout with his rod and line, he had a permit, and his need must surely excuse him for his unorthodox method.

As he gutted the fish he felt a sudden exultation. He had never guddled a trout from the river before, and it had worked, just as Tomkin had told him. Tomkin had spent a good deal of his youth poaching. He was now a reformed character as the colonel would not tolerate anything else, but he still remembered the old ways, and told them to Paddy Joe, not as a way of life, but as tales to wile away odd moments, when they sat together in friendly companionship polishing the hunters' saddles.

Loneliness was returning. Paddy Joe pushed memory away, and looked along the river bank. There was a small shelf, just round the corner, where the river had channelled into a rocky outcrop. It was sandy floored and protected by trees and would give shelter. It would be possible to light a fire and cook the trout. No one had passed since Paddy Joe had started his journey. He would have to be careful, lest the smoke attract attention. He collected dry kindling and lit the fire, adding larger pieces of wood until it blazed. He always carried matches in his rucksack, safely inside a tin, guarding them against damp. He speared the trout on his knife and held it over the flames. It was not the best method of cooking, but it would have to do. He thought, as he shared the half raw, half charred flesh with Storm, that he had tasted nothing half so good for a long time. He had never been so hungry in his life.

The trout, shared between them, was only a mouthful after all, and it looked far smaller gutted than it had before. The head and tail accounted for so much of it. It was soon only a memory. Paddy Joe buried the remnants, using the broad blade of his knife to dig in the soft shingle, and carefully hid all traces of his meal. He found his mug and drank, and then took water to douse the fire, stamping the ashes and spreading them. He used his hands to dig leaf mould which he scattered over the shelf, hiding all sign of a fire, and he also used his knife to scrape the earth where Storm had left two pawmarks. He looked around him. Nothing showed that they had ever been there. It was time to go.

Time had passed swiftly while they had been eating, and the light had changed, so that dawn and softness of sky and air were only a memory and the sun was bright and the shadows etched black on the ground. Far away the hum and whine of cars breasting the hill grew and died and grew again. There were people about. He must get away. As far away as possible. Right away, so that no one could find him. For the first time in his life he longed for darkness and was afraid of the light, and wondered if he had better hide till nightfall.

But nothing travelled at night, and he might find help if he went on. He thought of the hobbits, riding out alone, with the Night Riders following them. He had never thought that he too would know what it was like to feel hunted and unwanted, alone and on the run.

It was a chilling thought, and his spirits sank again. He must get away. The words chanted through his mind as he walked. I must get away. I must get away. I must get away, as one foot followed the other along the narrow path and Storm plodded on, now bewildered by their adventure, but following because he would never leave Paddy Joe.

I must get away. I must get away. I must get away. But how?

Chapter Four

Day meant danger. It meant people waking and seeing him, and it meant Martha finding he was gone. He wondered again what she would do. Would she telephone Mr Throstle? Or would she look aimlessly for him in summerhouse and storeroom, under beds and in his secret places? Or would she simply assume he had got up early and gone walking with Storm for a last farewell to the house and garden before they took him away?

Paddy Joe could not guess. He only knew that when Mr Throstle's clerk came, someone would realise that he had run away, and then the whole relentless machinery of civilisation would start up. People would be looking for him.

He wound his watch. Time was important. It was just after seven-thirty and Martha would be waking. So would the towns and villages. He must leave the river. It was necessary to get as far away as possible, ensuring that no trail led to him, no clue betrayed him, no man knew anything about him that might make him sit up suddenly as he read a newspaper and think,

"That's the boy I saw yesterday. He's unmistakable, with that big dog."

It would be easier to lose himself without Storm. The magnificent Alsatian often made heads turn towards them. There was no way of disguising him. No matter what Paddy Joe did to himself, Storm would remain remarkable. He looked at the dog now, savouring him intensely, as if he were tasting him, looking at the powerful shoulders, the wise alert head, the prick ears that spoke as eloquently as the warm brown eyes that watched Paddy Joe eagerly, delighting in this un-expected adventure, and in having the boy's company without the unwelcome break of school hours. Paddy Joe reached out his hand to touch his dog, and then, remembering that if they were caught, the dog would have to die, he gripped Storm so tightly that the dog struggled to free himself. The next second, impelled by delirium brought on by morning and the fresh wind that was flying towards them from the southwest, clouding the sky, the dog leaped at Paddy Joe. In a moment they were rolling together in play, breathlessly romping, until Paddy Joe remembered that today play was something that must be forgotten, and that even the grass broken down by their weight might bring danger. Any dog that hunted along this side of the river might pick up their scent. He had been stupid.

He washed his face in the shallows, and drank a little of the water in his cupped hands. Beside him, the dog lapped greedily. The trout had made them thirsty.

When both had finished, Paddy Joe looked around him. He knew this part of the river well. It swooped rapidly round a bend and thrust its way over a small rocky face, and from there dipped and surged over shelving steps until it found the gash where the rock cracked, and roared over the fall into the little gorge below. Tomkin liked the gorge, which gave ample cover and let them see without being seen, and walk without being heard, every footfall drowned in the din of the racing water.

Here the river bank steepened. They climbed it to the top, and Paddy Joe saw to his relief that they were beside the pony field. These were bred by an old lady who was a famous judge of horses, and who owned High Glee, the champion stallion that had won Best in Show

44

at the last Royal Show. He and Grandee had gone to the show together. It was not a thought to remember. They would never go anywhere together again.

Tomkin had told him that horses and donkeys never spoiled their grazing. In a big field, they only soiled the edges near the hedge. That was how gipsies and horse thieves knew where horses were pastured. They searched the field edge for droppings. Paddy Joe climbed the gate and Storm vaulted it. The boy walked along the hedge to see for himself if what Tomkin had said were true. It was true, and here once more he could foul his scent and smother his shoes until no dog could trace him, or know that the smell on the track was from anything but horses.

Storm was frisky. He romped absurdly, gambolling like a pup. Paddy Joe left him, hoping that temptation would be too strong for the dog. The droppings were fresh and warm, and the ponies looked inquisitively towards them. They were lazy, and resumed their feeding. Paddy Joe wished so hard that he thought he might burst. If only there were magic, and he had a ring he might touch, and bring help. Or a lamp he might rub to invoke a genie who would do his bidding and carry both of them far away, out of reach of the men who were so determined that he and Storm should be parted.

Wishing was useless. He had just given up when Storm did just what he hoped. Temptation proved too strong, and the Alsatian was rolling in the mounds of horse dung, plastering them over feet and body, until he was as mucky as any pooch that wandered the streets from dawn to dusk with no one to tend him. The dog stood up, and looked sheepishly at Paddy Joe, expecting a chiding. Paddy Joe dared not praise him, lest he thought that in future such behaviour was to be tolerated. Tomkin had told him always to be consistent, and Storm knew very well that on normal occasions such habits brought both annoyance, and a bath. Paddy Joe contented himself now with saying "Oh Storm," but it was hard to say it as if he meant it, because the muck hid most of the dog's colouring, and also masked his scent completely. He had longed for the dog to roll.

He walked across the field, flicking his fingers to the Alsatian, who followed him, quite content to smell of pony, feeling comfortably messy. The dog stopped once to sniff at a rabbit hole, and savour the enticing smell that came from it, but Paddy Joe called him on. Time was passing too quickly, and he did not know how to get away from the area. He needed a lift, but now that Storm was so filthy no one would want him near. The boy sighed. One problem solved only seemed to lead to yet another that had no solution. It was like going round and round in a maze. It was impossible. Storm, hearing the sigh, thrust a cold nose into Paddy Joe's hand. It was impossible to be downhearted with such good company. There would be a solution, somewhere, somehow. Paddy Joe began to whistle under his breath. If he whistled Greensleeves, which was Tomkin's tune, perhaps he would begin to think like Tomkin, who could solve everything.

There was a great deal to solve. To start with, he was still hungry, and so was Storm. He shared the bar of chocolate with the dog, but it was no more than a mouthful and did not ease the pangs that were becoming stronger with every minute. It was too early for blackberries and in any case Storm was not likely to eat those. There was no more time to fish. Time was vital; time to get as far away as possible before the daytime folk were about their business.

The field of ponies led, by way of a stile, to a field of sheep. Paddy Joe was suddenly aware that the sheep were milling and bleating, running senselessly every whichway, seeming not to know what was happening, or where to find safety. Tomkin had taught him to observe all animals; to see a horse stare prick-eared in the ditch and look for the cause of his curiosity; to see a pigeon fly straight and suddenly change direction, startled by a man below him, a man who might carry a weapon; to see sheep moiling patter-scatter, and search for the creature that was alarming them.

A moment later, he saw the cause of the trouble. A fox was running among the sheep, a gaunt beast, obviously ravenously hungry, trying for an easy kill. There was no time to think, no time to consider whether he was wise or unwise. Paddy Joe was country bred and to turn his back was unthinkable. He climbed the stile, and whistled to Storm. He pointed.

"Get him then. Drive him off."

Storm sniffed the rank pungent scent which overlaid the smell of sheep. Fox smell drove him mad, and he raced against the wind, his fur ruffled by unseen fingers, his mouth open, his tongue lolling with joy. He angled among the flock, and the beasts thought he was another enemy and increased their din. The air was horrid with fear, with terror bleat and panic call, as ewes cried to their lambs and the lambs, now well grown, raced for shelter to their mothers, who were the only comfort they knew.

Storm met the fox, head to head, growling his anger. The fox, having been busy trying to single a lame lamb and run it down and kill it, bridled with fury and leaped for Storm's throat. The dog jumped aside and ran in again, his teeth raking the fox's pointed jaunty ear. A pulsebeat later, they were rolling together, fighting in a mixture of snapping teeth and snarling voice and bite and rake and claw.

The noise was so great that the man who approached

Paddy Joe and spoke made the boy jump, and wheel, his brown eyes wide and startled.

"What the devil's going on?"

The man was obviously the shepherd. The two collies beside him were trembling with eagerness, but sat, obedient to his signal, waiting with tensed muscles for him to give the word to drive away the intruder.

"There's a fox among your sheep. I sent my dog in to chase it off. I couldn't leave it there." Paddy Joe's voice was anxious, and his eyes stared up at the man. Suppose he asked questions that Paddy Joe couldn't answer? Suppose there had already been an announcement about him on the radio?

"I've been hunting that fox for a week," the shepherd said, relaxing. He had been unable to see the two beasts, and thought two dogs were after his sheep. The fox had torn himself free. Storm raced in again, determined to finish his enemy, and Paddy Joe was bothered. The dog had a gash on his shoulder and his chest was covered with blood.

"Call your dog off, if he'll come. Old Red Ruin will run, and I'd not like your chap to be hurt bad," the shepherd said, and Paddy Joe whistled. He was afraid that Storm would not obey, but Storm knew that he must. He broke away, the shepherd yelled and threw a stone, and the fox limped off, lagleg, panting, brush down, defeated. He squeezed through the hedge and was gone.

"I wanted a lame lamb out for treatment," the shepherd said, "I'm taking him into town to the vet, as it's my day for marketing."

Storm limped back to Paddy Joe. His foot was also torn, and that was a new worry, as how could he walk far with a lame leg?

"Your dog had better see the vet too," the man added. He caught Paddy Joe's worried glance.

"I'll pay for him. One good turn . . ." The shepherd smiled reassuringly. He sent his two dogs in to single the lamb, and Paddy Joe watched them work, now one heading the lamb, now the other, approaching, crouching, waiting, obedient to every whistled signal, dogs and master working in complete accord until the lamb was brought to the shepherd who caught it with his crook and lifted it.

"My Land-Rover's in the lay-by. Come on, boy. Your dog needs treatment."

Paddy Joe followed. Storm limped beside him, but when Paddy Joe stopped to look at the dog, and to see the extent of his injury the Alsatian wagged an ardent tail and licked the boy's face, which was total reassurance.

The Land-Rover had once been grey, but it was now so covered in mud that its colour was lost in a general khaki coating. The soft top had several gashes in it, and one door was missing. Paddy Joe wondered how on earth anyone could be allowed to drive it, in a country where vehicles were tested every three years for road worthiness.

"I don't use it on the road," the shepherd said, following Paddy Joe's glance. "I bring the dogs out to the field in it. The farm's just along the lane. I've a better vehicle for going to market."

The two collies were already inside. The lamb was laid on a piece of sacking. It bleated for its mother, who came to the field edge and answered, her misery apparent. Her forlorn wails drowned the sound of the starting engine.

"He's grown up, and she'll soon forget him," the shepherd said, as he noticed Paddy Joe watching her. "Jump in."

"My dog's mucky," Paddy Joe said.

"So's that lamb. Farmers are used to muck. Come

on, boy. I want to eat before I go off, and I'll be bound you wouldn't say no to a second breakfast."

" I didn't have much for my first," Paddy Joe said, before he could stop himself. He groaned inside his head. He would have to be more careful. Words seemed to slip out by themselves sometimes and the last thing he wanted to do was cause comment.

"On holiday?" the shepherd asked.

"Sort of," Paddy Joe said. He tried desperately to find something else to add, something that wouldn't give him away, but his mind seemed to have stopped working. He played with all kinds of ideas but they were much too complicated, and he would have to remember everything he invented. It would be too easy to be confused and tell a different story each time and people might meet each other, compare notes, and begin to wonder.

Luckily the shepherd's mind was filled with his own affairs.

"Does a boy good to get away on his own. Must have sensible parents," the man said approvingly. "I used to rough it for weeks, out on the moors near where I lived as a boy. Did me a world of good. Parents cosset their kids far too much these days."

Paddy Joe relaxed. The man was obviously not wondering about him or his dog. The Land-Rover turned into a side lane, and bumped and lurched over a rutted track that had never been surfaced. The centre was green grass and ragwort-dotted, and the edges of the road were deep tracks that dropped away into the tangled ditch. Storm, looking out eagerly, wagged his tail continuously, wafting a rich odour towards Paddy Joe, who began to wish that the dog was not quite so close to him.

"Here we are," the shepherd said.

Here was a big house, black and white timber

fronted, and moulded with time. It seemed to have settled on its foundations, brooding deep amid the trees. A new brick wing added an ugly note. Beyond it was a white cottage with a thatched roof and a garden that would have stopped Grandee in her tracks, and sent her to the doorway begging for cuttings. Lavender bushes formed a thick short hedge, and brilliant flowers vied with one another to catch the sun. The Land-Rover drew up at the cottage gate.

"I'm back, and fair hungry enough to eat you and the kids as a starter," the shepherd called, and a tumble of small children came racing towards him, and then stood still, abashed, fingers in their mouths, when they saw Paddy Joe.

"This lad's dog chased off old Red Ruin for us," the shepherd said, as his wife came to the door. She was as small and fair as he was tall and dark, and they provided extreme contrast. Two of the children were tiny delicate creatures, the three others were sturdy as four-month lambs, and brown-faced and independent, for all their very few years. Paddy Joe followed them inside.

"Then he's more than welcome." The shepherd's wife set down a bowl of porridge and fetched another plate and laid another place. The kitchen was full of friendly bustle, the children pushing to sit at the big table, a cat suckling four kittens on a cushion-padded basket weave chair, a dog sprawled out on the hearth. This dog was not a collie, but a lurcher, lean and muscular. He beat his tail on the floor, and then saw Storm, who had followed Paddy Joe into the room.

"Quiet," Paddy Joe said. "Sit."

Storm sat. The lurcher approached the bigger dog cautiously, his hind legs bent, his tail between his knees. The Alsatian wagged his tail. The lurcher relaxed and returned to his place on the hearth.

"Torry knows who's boss," the shepherd said. "He does that to the collies, because they're top dogs around here. Can't work without them."

The porridge plates were cleared and a dish of eggs and bacon and mushrooms and tomatoes was divided up among the family.

"Everything here's laid on," the shepherd said. "Pigs for bacon, and eggs from our own chickens. The wife grows tomatoes in the porch as well as in the little greenhouse, and the mushrooms came from the field by the river. Nothing like living in the country. D'you live in the country, boy? I should think you do, seeing you knew enough to drive the fox out of my sheep field."

Paddy Joe's mouth was full, so that he contented himself with nodding. Nobody seemed to expect any more, and he was glad to sit back and not think. He was feeling very tired. He had never stayed up the whole night before, without the chance to sleep on in the morning.

The shepherd gave food to Storm. He had been watching Paddy Joe and seeing more than the boy thought, but he decided not to press the lad. He'd done him a right good turn and maybe there was nothing in his suspicions. He seemed a nice boy, nicely brought up, and well spoken. There couldn't be any harm in him.

The eldest boy was talking to Paddy Joe.

"I'm a Wolf Cub. I've got both eyes open now," he said proudly.

"I'm a Scout. I was a Wolf Cub," Paddy Joe said.

"Are you taking a badge?" the shepherd's wife asked. She had cleared the dishes away and was pouring thick milky drinks into the children's beakers.

"Sort of," Paddy Joe said again. He was wondering how on earth he was going to fend off questions without being rude. It was far more difficult than he had imagined.

"Be like our Nellie's Derek, taking his initiative test," the shepherd said lazily. He had eaten an enormous meal. Paddy Joe wondered how on earth he could eat so much. "He had to get from London to Edinburgh on 50p, live off the land, and not spend more than he needed. He came home with 25p, which I reckoned pretty good. Is that what you're doing, boy?"

"Sort of," Paddy Joe said again. It sounded a very good idea, but he needed to take it, look at it, shake it up and stand it on its head so that he could see all kinds of snags, before he adopted it. He was worried about his lapse. He hadn't meant to say he'd had hardly any breakfast. This time it didn't matter, but it might have done. In future he intended to think hard before he did anything at all. In which case he might well end up doing nothing at all. Life was too confusing.

"We must get to the vet, and then on to the town," the shepherd said. "Tell you what, boy. Would you like to make your camp here? You could sleep in the big barn if it got wet. There might be a few rats for company but your dog could take care of those. I owe you something. Red Ruin's clever, and he's had two of my lambs this year."

It was very tempting. Somewhere to stay, and people to talk to, and perhaps feed him. It would be wonderful to belong but it was far too close to home. There were people near who knew him, and visitors to the farm might recognise Storm. Paddy Joe sighed and shook his head.

"I'd like to," he said wistfully. He remembered the initiative test. "Only somehow, it makes it too easy."

"Mebbe you're right. We'll be away, then." The shepherd added to his wife. "Expect me when you see me."

"I will that, and see you come home on two legs and sober, and not in Tom Lackem's lorry this time," his wife said, and from her tone Paddy Joe could tell that she meant it.

The shepherd laughed.

"I'll not even wet my whistle," he promised.

"That'll be the day," his wife said, and picked up the baby, who was hitching himself along on his bottom down the garden path. The front door slammed behind her.

"Women!" the shepherd said, as he started the engine. "You can't live wi' 'em and you can't live wi'out 'em. Make the most of being young, lad. It won't last."

There seemed no kind of reply to that. Paddy Joe contented himself with watching the fields speed by. Every mile was taking him to safety. Every mile driven meant no trail was being left for a dog to find. If only they didn't put out a radio or TV appeal. If only the shepherd never discovered that a boy and an Alsatian dog was missing. If only he didn't connect them with Paddy Joe and Storm. Paddy Joe had told him that their names were Pat Jones and Riff.

The vet's house was big and old and comfortable, standing in its own grounds. Dogs were penned in cages, and they leaped at the wire and barked as Paddy Joe came in with Storm, followed by the shepherd carrying his sick lamb. Paddy Joe wondered briefly if he might leave Storm here for safe keeping and return home, as it seemed unlikely he would be able to keep himself and the dog fed until the colonel returned from his fishing trip. The vet might understand. And he might not. Also there was the thought of Mr Throstle and the Boys' Home in the town. Paddy Joe decided to follow his own way and take happenings as they came.

The fox and the shepherd was one piece of luck. Perhaps there always was luck for travellers. Perhaps the happenings in *The Lord of the Rings* weren't so unusual. After all, he had met the shepherd right at the beginning just as the hobbits had met Tom Bombadil. Somehow, it made things easier to keep comparing with something familiar. *The Lord of the Rings* was the last link with Grandee. They had been reading it the night before her accident, and she had laughed with him over some of the funny incidents, and sighed with him over the sad ones. It made her seem closer, and as if she had not really gone for ever, but had left him briefly, to sleep in another room, where he must not disturb her. It was a comforting thought.

The vet's waiting-room was bare, and almost empty. A grey-haired woman sat near the door, a shivering pup on her knee.

"He was bitten by a bigger dog yesterday," she explained. "He's scared of your Alsatian."

"Sit," said Paddy Joe, and as Storm obeyed the shepherd nodded approvingly.

"I can see you've both been trained by a good master," he said and patted the dogs. Suddenly Paddy Joe found himself telling the shepherd about the colonel and about his riding lessons and about Tomkin, who could charm a trout from the stream, or a partridge from a furrow, or a pheasant from a tree. He wished Tomkin were here, so that he could see the familiar lop-lipped grin, and feel the strength and comfort that the man generated. There was something about Tomkin that nobody could describe. All beasts trusted him, and he could gentle a wayward horse, or soothe a restive bull, or comfort an ailing cow. He had tamed almost every creature under the sun, from a tiny snarling weasel kit, to a fox that followed him like a dog, and a badger that ran to greet him, yickering with shrill pleasure. Tomkin and the colonel had fought together during the war and the man had saved the colonel's life. Even Storm, although Paddy Joe was his, and he was

Paddy Joe's, had a very firm affection for Tomkin, whom he greeted riotously, as opposed to the colonel, who was given a stately welcome.

The shepherd listened. Tomkin sounded a man after his own heart. No wonder the boy was well taught about the country and wildlife. He had happened on a miracle. There were very few men like Tomkin left. You needed a special kind of man for beasts. All beasts responded to extra care and attention, just like children, flowering in a climate of approval. Yet few men knew that, and a poor farmer was often jealous of a good one, not knowing that the good farmer spent his time and his care ensuring that his farm stock was as happy and comfortable and cared for as possible.

It was time to see the vet. They had been so busy talking that they had not seen the grey-haired woman go in with her pup.

"That's a nasty gash," the vet said, "Is he fighting other dogs?"

"He chased Red Ruin off my flock this morning. The fox did that," the shepherd said.

"He never fights other dogs," Paddy Joe added indignantly. "I've trained him not to. Up," he added to Storm.

The dog jumped on to the table and held up the gashed paw.

"I'll be damned," the vet said. "I wish all my patients were like you!"

Storm sat quietly while his cuts were bathed and ointment put on them, and he was given an injection, in case he had picked up some infection from the bites.

"One good thing, he doesn't need any stitches. Don't let him run too far or too much on that leg of his." The vet patted Storm. "You're a fine fellow. You need a bath, though, don't you?"

"He's only just done that," Paddy Joe said. "He'll

get bathed as soon as we get home." It was the absolute truth. The only trouble was that Paddy Joe had no idea when that would be.

"I'll give you some lunch, boy, and set you on your way," the shepherd said. "I think chasing off Red Ruin showed plenty of initiative. So I can safely give you a bit of a reward without upsetting your test."

"On an initiative test, are you?" the vet asked. "Scouting's a fine thing. I'll wish you luck."

He handed over a small tube of ointment to Paddy Joe.

"If you aren't going home at once, you may need that for your dog. And if those bites look sore, see that you get him to a vet."

Paddy Joe walked outside while they discussed the lame lamb. He was not yet on his own again, but he very soon would be, and he had another problem. Storm was limping badly, and whatever they did, they could not go far. He would have to find somewhere to shelter. The last signpost had said that they were twenty-five miles away from home. This was strange country. Paddy Joe sighed. He was not at all sure that adventure was half so much fun as all the books made out. This time, he had been lucky. Suppose his luck gave out?

He couldn't be worse off. And each day was a day gained, and a day longer for Storm. Each day brought the colonel's return closer, only the hours passed so slowly.

Paddy Joe hugged his knees as he waited. Above his head the sky brooded, dark with angry cloud, threatening bad weather. A sheet of lightning flashed and died, leaving the world drained of colour. Paddy Joe watched the sky, and his own thoughts were as tossed and tumbled as the tormented clouds that ran before a wind that was shivering the trees.

Chapter Five

When Paddy Joe left the shepherd, he felt more alone than ever. They had a meal at the Ploughman's Arms, where he was fed steak and kidney pudding, with cabbage and mashed potatoes, and a big helping of apple pie and cream, followed by cheese and biscuits. Storm was given a bone to gnaw on the gravel outside the window, as he was far too dirty to come inside. So long as he could see Paddy Joe, the dog was quite contented.

"It's good country over in the hills," the shepherd said, before he drove back to pick up his lamb, which had had an abscess that the vet was going to treat while the shepherd went to market. "Tell any of the farmers there that you're a friend of Willie Brakewell, and they'll give you a barn to sleep in at night, and help you on your way. How far have you got to go?"

"It's not distance, it's time," Paddy Joe said. "I've got to last out as long as I'm able."

"Don't be too cussed about it," said Willie Brakewell. "If you get too wet and cold and hungry ring your dad. Will he come for you?"

Paddy Joe nodded, as that was not quite so untrue as saying yes. He wished with all his heart that it were true, and then he remembered Tomkin and the colonel.

"If he can't, Tomkin will come, he always does," he said. That was true, so long as Tomkin was at home and not in Scotland, and the shepherd drove off, quite sure that all was well with Paddy Joe and that his suspicion that there was something amiss was just wullywondering, a niggling doubt that was now at rest.

Paddy Joe looked about him. The wooded country was only a memory. Here the land was bleak and hilly and unfamiliar, bold moors rising stark against the sky, scarred by gullies and ravines that sheltered stunted trees and malformed bushes. There was no cover on the slopes. The clouds massed angrily, lit by a sullen sulphur glow. Paddy Joe dared not walk far, not with Storm's torn shoulder and bitten leg. But they needed food and they needed shelter. Perhaps in the tree-lined gullies there would be water and caves. This was limestone country, the shepherd had said, and where there was limestone there were caves, and pot-holes. He would have to be very careful.

The wind sharpened, chilling him, and its uneasy sigh deepened to an uncanny scream as it surged over the hills and winged through the telegraph wires, and whined over the sparse tussocky grass where a few shaggy and dirty sheep grazed unhappily, keeping in the hollows to avoid the wind's cold caress. Dust flung from the road stung legs and faces. Storm stopped to rub a paw over smarting eyes, and Paddy Joe blinked away the tears that sprang up in his own, stinging with grit. Walking was misery, and to add to his worries, thunder rumbled ominously in the distance and lightning flicked across the sky, leaving the world uncannily dark after its sudden blinding brilliance.

The little shop at the edge of the greystone village street was a haven. Paddy Joe looked about him as he entered. Wool and hardware jostled food and sweets, and a small elderly woman, her spectacles on a cord round her neck, watched him suspiciously. Storm sat outside the door, his ears pricked uneasily. He was not afraid of thunder, but he did not like it and the surly grumbling now echoed continuously, while flashes of lightning sparked between the lowering clouds.

"Well?" the shopkeeper said sharply. She did not like boys, nor did she like dogs and Storm was so large that he could eye her through the top of the half-glassed door. Tear you apart, Alsatians did, dangerous beasts, the woman thought. Her fear made her snap, and Paddy Joe, worried by her unfriendliness, hurried over his purchases.

He bought a tin of dog food and a tin opener, which took more money than he expected. He handed over the coins reluctantly. He had so little left. A sliced loaf cost more than he had imagined, too, and he bought half a pound of butter. Nearly all his money was gone already and there seemed almost nothing to show for it.

"Hurry up, boy," the woman said. "Or you'll never get home before the storm breaks. Staying with friends, are you? I've not seen you before. Or come from a car?"

Paddy Joe nodded, unable to answer questions. If she thought he was with someone in a car she would forget him promptly, as soon as he had gone. In such a small place she was bound to know everyone and could catch him out. He hastily spent more of his small hoard of coins on a piece of cheddar cheese. Bread and cheese would keep him going for a day or two, even if it was scarcely an exciting diet. Storm's food was more difficult. A tin of dogmeat usually only lasted one meal. Paddy Joe had already spent more than two-thirds of his money. He watched as the shopkeeper put his purchases in a bag, and anxiously counted his change.

He thanked the woman and walked out into a world that had darkened to midnight black. His spirits were as bleak as the sky. Initiative was all very well, but how could they both survive for another eight days? Paddy Joe was so miserably engrossed in his grim thoughts that the rain took him by surprise. He began to run, and Storm bounded eagerly beside him. They needed shelter.

The road was bordered by a drystone wall. Beyond the wall was a canal, and along the canal was a low tunnel, formed by a humpback bridge that carried a narrow road. The centre of the tunnel would be dry and it was safer than sheltering under trees in a storm. A tree might be struck by lightning. They reached the archway just as the first splatter of rain became a torrential downpour.

Paddy Joe sat down with his back against the dank stone wall, and the dog crouched beside him. Rain lanced from the sky, slashing into the water with an uncanny hissing sound. Rain bounded on the towpath and drummed on the road above their heads. The world was alive with sound. Lightning flickered and flashed on the hilltops that bounded the horizon, thunder rolled and drummed in their ears, echoing hollowly in the cavernous archway. The day had vanished. Sunshine was a distant memory from another time and another life, and Paddy Joe shivered, cooled by the chill air that came off the water. He curled up close to Storm, garnering warmth from the dog.

A car crossed the bridge, changing gear noisily, and Storm, startled, lifted his head and growled. Paddy Joe wondered bleakly where they could spend the night. If the rain did not ease, they would be forced to stay where they were. At least the ground was dry and they were out of sight of the road, but they could be seen by the boats that came along the canal, and the people on them might notice and wonder. Thinking was exhausting, as worry added to worry. Paddy Joe was tired out. He had been up all night. He dozed, and Storm kept watch, his dark eyes brilliant, his pointed ears alert for unusual sounds.

The rain did not ease till late evening. Paddy Joe woke, his legs stiff and aching. Everything felt strange, and he wondered about it until he realised that the noise had ceased. There was only a thin drip of water, sliding from the brickwork of the archway, and the murmur of a slight breeze, rustling the bushes. The air was fresh and clean, the ground new-washed, and the smell of wet grass strong. Storm licked Paddy Joe's face, and stretched himself and sat up, sighing deeply. The dog was thirsty, and when Paddy Joe walked to the archway opening, Storm followed and drank from a puddle. Paddy Joe was thirsty too, but the canal water was dark and muddy, and debris floated on a scummy surface. He dared not drink from it.

They needed a safe place for the night. The canal flowed sluggishly, hidden from the road by the wall. Safety lay along the towpath, where they would get warning of approaching boats, as the engine noises carried plainly, and they could keep out of sight. The path was overgrown and wet. Long grass soaked Paddy Joe's legs, and once moving carelessly, he tripped over a hidden rock and fell and stung his hands on some nettles. The stings smarted, and he found a dock leaf, and spat and rubbed the dock on his palm, but it made little difference.

Thirst niggled, and his mouth was dry. The dirty water was foul and a smell of rottenness came from it. Paddy Joe longed for the clear run and sparkle of the river at home. A solitary swan, its feathers dingy with grime, swam aimlessly. A giant rat ran along the far bank and dived into the water, the dull splash sending widening ripples that plashed softly against the concrete rim at the edge of the bank.

The towpath continued to the edge of the hill, and Paddy Joe to his surprise found that he was on an aqueduct. Below him were fields in which cattle grazed, and a road, busy with cars that defied the dusk with brilliant headlights that swathed the walls bordering the road. Paddy Joe had never seen water on top of a bridge before, and he stopped, intrigued, to examine the enormous iron trough that carried the canal and the path beside it. It was difficult to imagine that boats soared along here, high above the road, and once, even, had been drawn by plodding horses. It was strange to think that the people in cars on the road, looking up, would see boats riding high above them, suspended in air. Paddy Joe wondered how the bridge had been built, all those years ago, before men had bulldozers and cranes and pneumatic drills. The stone piers must be well over a hundred feet high and the aqueduct spanned dizzily across the gash in the hills, so that everything below was dwarfed and unreal, toy cows in toy fields and toy cars spinning along a toy road.

Beyond the fields the aqueduct ended in a tunnel. Perhaps he could spend the night inside. It would be dry and sheltered. But inside, the walls ran with moisture and the air was foetid, stale with mould, and disuse, and breathing was difficult. It was necessary to hurry through, feeling the way by holding on to the slimy brickwork, afraid of tripping and falling, afraid, suddenly, that the towpath might have collapsed and that instead of solid ground, there would only be the dark water, under which unknown horrors lurked.

Paddy Joe slowed down as wings brushed his face. A bat had flown through the darkness and the ghost noise of its passing left his heart racing, while Storm growled softly. Storm was comfort, and Paddy Joe relied on the dog's quick sense to keep them safe. If only the tunnel would end. He began to regret that he had entered it. How far did it go? He could see no shimmer of light from the other end. Suppose it was blind, or blanked off, or there had been a fall which blocked it completely? It would have been wiser to wait till morning. Suppose there was firedamp in the tunnel, or marsh gas, or were they the same thing? Miners died from gas, and the tunnel was just like a mine, delving deep into the hill. Suppose the other end blocked while he was inside? Suppose he were trapped? Paddy Joe began to run and immediately tripped and fell headlong, one hand trailing in the icy water.

He picked himself up, and took a deep breath, then wished that he hadn't. He was deep inside the hill, silence all round him. The trickling water made soft gurgling noises, and there were no other sounds but his own breathing and that of the dog. Paddy Joe reassured himself by feeling the soft fur round Storm's neck, and Storm butted his muzzle into the boy's knee. He did not like the tunnel either.

Paddy Joe began to count his paces. One. Two. Three. Four. Surely he must soon see light, and see the end of the tunnel. He would have liked to use his torch but it was inside the rucksack and he was afraid he might spill some of his few stores into the water if he looked for it. He was hungry, and he was thirsty, and he was tired. Perhaps if he tried walking to the tune of a marching song deep inside his head, he might conquer fear.

He tried marching to the tune of Men of Harlech, but he had forgotten the words, and when he hummed the song the echo was so ghostly that he stopped, afraid that someone might hear him. If only the tunnel would end.

The tunnel curved, and as he rounded the bend, he saw, to his relief, that the end was in sight, a round hole in the darkness, in which five stars were framed. Night had come while he was walking through. The gleam was welcome and encouraged him, but now the towpath was uneven, worn by time, and broken in places, so that he had to walk cautiously. It seemed hours before the arch of light grew, and the world beyond revealed itself.

The hillside sloped steeply away at their feet. Paddy

Joe gulped in clean air, aware as never before of the need to breathe deeply, and of the difference between foul air and good air. He breathed until his lungs felt ready to burst, thankful to be out of the dark tunnel, even though night was upon him.

A bat flittered briefly and was gone. Water, nearby, fought its way down the hillside, and Paddy Joe tracked the sound, pushing through overgrown bushes that were sodden with rain, until he came to a small fall that burst over a rocky face, and sparkled in the moonlight as it fell towards the distant river. The canal vanished behind a lockgate that held the water in thrall. Paddy Joe knelt and drank deeply, slaking a thirst that had bedevilled him for hours.

Darkness loomed from the sky and the moon was a ghost of herself, giving little comfort. Ragged clouds drifted over her shimmering face. Paddy Joe looked around him. The dark gape of a cave, half-hidden by bushes, faced him. He knelt on the wet grass and unpacked his rucksack. There was just enough light to see. He found the torch. It needed a new battery and this was another problem. He did not like the thought of being without light. He flashed the torch at the cave entrance. It was small, but would hold the two of them. The floor was stony and gritty with dust, but it was quite dry. It offered sanctuary for the night.

It was good to stretch tired arms and ease tired legs. It was good to lie quiet for a brief moment and watch the ghost moon strengthen until moonlight shivered on the waterfall and reflected in the raindrops on the trees, so that leaf and stem and flower sparkled. The wind was only a whisper, gentling the grasses, nodding the tips of branches, warming the chilled air.

There was light enough now to open Storm's tin of meat. Paddy Joe cleared a patch of rock and turned the food out on to it, afraid that the dog might cut his mouth on the tin's sharp edges. The dog began to eat, gulping greedily, satisfying his hunger. There was light enough to find knife and butter, and take four slices of the cut loaf and some of the cheese and make sandwiches that were food fit for heroes. Nothing had ever tasted so good. Not even the trout that morning. It had been so long since lunch. Paddy Joe felt strength come back to him as he ate.

Storm licked the rock clean and licked his whiskers and his chops. He walked outside and smelled the night. No threat there. He came back and flung himself on the ground and Paddy Joe knew there was no danger outside in the dark. The dog was relaxed. If he had been worried by unseen threats he would have crouched with muscles tense and ears pricked, ready to growl a warning, ready to jump at man or beast, should either intrude.

Paddy Joe spread his sleeping bag, and climbed inside, pillowing his head on Storm's shoulder. It had been a long day, and he had not slept at all the night before. Within seconds, time had ceased to matter and he was deep in a dreamless sleep. Storm brooded, head on his paws, listening, alert, watchful. The moon set. Darkness shadowed the cave, and beyond, the busy road became quiet, lights went out in the village, and only the hoot owl, hunting hungrily, flew on slow beating wings, a phantom bird of night.

Chapter Six

Storm was growling. Paddy Joe sat up, anxious. Day had taken him by surprise and sunshine flooded the cave. A long shadow lay across him, and the Alsatian's ruff was bristling. Paddy Joe looked up and sat up, startled, as one of the biggest men he had ever seen bent to look at him.

"It's all right, lad. Tell your dog I don't mean no 'arm," the man said. "Tom Vence never 'urt nobody in 'is life, and 'e's not starting now."

"Quiet, Storm," Paddy Joe said, and the dog was silent, but he remained alert, ready to protect his master, not taking the newcomer on trust.

Paddy Joe crawled out of his sleeping bag, feeling at a considerable disadvantage. His clothes were creased and his hair rumpled; he was hungry and thirsty and felt unbearably scruffy. He was not happy about the man who faced him, sitting on the sawn-off stump of a tree, with an alert little terrier beside him. The scout beret was on top of Paddy Joe's rucksack and he saw the man look at it.

"Camping out's good for lads," the man observed. "What would you say to some rabbit pie, eh, lad? Reckon I've enough for two, and enough rabbit left over for your dog to share with Spot. You go and tidy up, and come back 'ere. I don't mean no 'arm. Don't see many folk to talk to, any road. It's nice to have a chat now and then. And I reckon you could do with some company too, eh, lad?"

Paddy Joe nodded. He still felt uneasy, but as he

slipped down the hill towards the water, the man began to unpack his haversack, and whistled to himself tunelessly. The terrier rubbed up against her master, catlike, and his face creased into a gentle smile as he rubbed her head between the ears.

"Who says you're the best ratter in these parts?" the man asked her. "Yer the best ratter anywhere, my beauty."

The terrier leaped up and licked his face eagerly. Paddy Joe relaxed. Tomkin always said a man gave himself away when he was alone with his dog. If the dog behaved well with the man, the man was all right. Had the dog backed away, or cowered, then there would have been trouble. The man would have been untrustworthy.

The water was cold, and Paddy Joe was wide awake by the time he had combed his hair and tidied himself. The slabs of rabbit pie made his mouth water, and Storm watched eagerly as the man took a parcel of meat and divided it between the terrier and the Alsatian.

"I never was a Scout meself," Tom Vence observed. "It's a great life for a lad tho' and good for city kids to get out in the country and live natural. Eat up, boy. You're all right?"

"I'm all right," Paddy Joe said, and bit into the pie with satisfaction. He remembered the shepherd. "Do you know Willie Brakewell?"

"Oh, aye, everyone knows Willie. Best sheepdog man there is in the whole of five counties. If you know Willie you're all right. Any farmer'll give you a place in his barn on a wet night. Just mention Willie."

"You like sleeping out?" Tom asked, after a long silence that was only broken by the sound of munching.

Paddy Joe nodded.

"I slep' out all my life," Tom said cheerfully. "Now I'm old, I got a little 'ut, and me and Spot sleep there.

It's dry and me bones ache these days. I'm well over seventy, lad. I got a job, keeping weeds down on the canal. Me dad did it too, in 'is time. A great one was me dad."

A butterfly danced over a willowherb flower, watched by both Spot and Storm. Sunshine brightened the canal, which lay below them, brought down by a flight of locks that Paddy Joe had not seen the night before. A proper staircase of locks, nine in a row. The water surged through the gates, leaking through the paddles, so that the whole reach was white with foam.

"I was a strong man in a circus once," Tom said. "Wouldn't credit it now, would yer? Used ter take on all comers at the County Fairs for threepence a time, and they got five shillings if they knocked me out. Only one man ever did, and he was a perliceman, a great big barrel of a fellow. Cor, I can feel that punch now." Tom rubbed his chin reflectively. He was enjoying talking. Company was rare, and he intended to make the most of it.

"You ain't got brothers and sisters?" he asked.

Paddy Joe shook his head.

"There was eight of us. Eight, and me dad only earned thirty shillings a week, but we never went 'ungry." Tom chuckled, a fat chuckle that shook his chest and the flabby paunch that hung over his trousers. He was a large man, the remains of a few red hairs clinging to his skull, and his blue eyes shone with laughter.

"You know why, lad?"

Paddy Joe shook his head again. He was beginning to enjoy listening.

"Me dad used to send us off to the blacksmith for the ends of the 'orse shoes. Iron bits cut off, about the size of a penny. And a bit of penny 'lastic from the village shop. Then 'e'd make a catapult. Out we'd go, on

71

moony nights when the wind was still, and me dad'd whistle, phwee, phwee, like a pheasant, and silly pheasant'd stick 'is 'ead out of a tree, and wham! Dad was a great shot wi' the catapult. We'd 'ave to go and get the bird, barefoot 'n all, nettles and thistles and prickles 'n all, or dad'd baste us wi' the buckle end of 'is belt, and prickles was better ner that. 'ad to watch out fer keeper too. Those pheasants tasted good."

"I've never tasted pheasant," Paddy Joe said.

"Not so many about now," Tom answered. "Though I could show you where hen's got her young in the wood down there. I never lived in a real 'ouse, lad, you imagine that? We lived in a wooden shack, down on the edge of the canal. Never knew what it were like to 'ave a dad wiv a proper job or a proper job meself, till lately when I started on the canal bank. Dad didn't like work. 'E only did it when 'e felt like it. You 'ad a dad what come 'ome every night to your mum?"

"My mum and dad died when I was a baby," Paddy Joe said.

Tom made a commiserating noise.

"All me mum and dad ever did was argue and 'it us," Tom said. "Yer niver 'eard anything like it. Mum could yell louder ner a frightened cock pheasant when she were angry, and she were often angry. 'I'll break damned jug over yer damned silly 'ead, you little idjut,' she'd say, and she would 'ave too, only jugs cost money. So she clouted us instead. Didn't do to argue with our mum. I left 'ome as soon as I were big enough. Went potato 'arvesting when I were twelve, and never lived at 'ome since. Couldn't do that these days, not at twelve, though its serprising what yer can do if yer try. You know, lad, there's two things I never did in all my life, I wished I 'ad. I've got two regrets, I'ave. I allus wanted a pig. Me dad 'ad a pig once. A big black cross-tempered thing it were too, and he reared it to be a big

72

'un. It fed us a lot of meals, did that pig. I allus wanted to rear me a pig. And I never 'ad a son. I never 'ad a pig. And I never 'ad a son. You don't want to live rough all your life, lad. You grow up and buy a little 'ouse and find yerself a job, a real job, wiv money coming in regular, every week, not now and then, like, and you git yerself a pig. There's summat satisfying about pigs. They don't know 'ow to rear them, no more. Me dad fed ours on swill and potato peelings and then, a fortnight before 'e killed it, all 'is money went on oatmeal fer the pig. Fatten up a treat on oatmeal, and yer can't beat the flavour. Bacon ain't got no flavour any more, not with all this modern feeding. They don't know 'ow to rear pigs."

He filled his mouth with rabbit pie and looked mournfully at Paddy Joe.

"There's lots of things changed," he said, swallowing and wiping his mouth with an enormous dark blue and rather dirty handkerchief. "No keepers any more. There's no fun poachin' if there's no keeper. Doin' keeper down, that were 'arf the fun. Now nobody sees yer, and there's not many left can tell yer 'ow hare runs in the furrow, or where the partridge coveys feed. Not many knows a lapwing from a magpie when it's flying."

"I know a man that does," Paddy Joe said. He wished that Tomkin were there, that he and the colonel would come up the hill, and end this adventure. It was beginning to be frightening. Only one day gone, and already he had spent most of his money, and Storm was limping from the cut on his paw.

"Your dog been fighting?" Tom Vence asked, as Storm moved stiffly towards the water to drink.

"He chased a fox from Willie Brakewell's sheep," Paddy Joe said. "I've got some ointment for his leg."

"I'm a dab 'and at looking after animals," Tom Vence said. "You got a clean 'ankie, and I'll bathe that for 'im and put the stuff on. I like looking after beasts. Sometimes the farmer lets me 'elp with 'is cows, and I can whisper a 'orse. You know about 'orse whisperers?"

Paddy Joe found the ointment and a handkerchief and shook his head.

"I can gentle a bad tempered 'orse as quick as maybe," Tom said. His hands moved carefully over Storm's leg. "I like 'orses. And they likes me. Get a nowty 'orse, and talk to 'im softlike, and 'e'll do anythink for yer."

Storm licked Tom's hand.

"See, beasts trust me. Once I 'ad a little foxcub, and 'e used ter foller me like a dog. 'e died, though. Vet said it was vitamins. 'e was near starving when I found 'im. Been living on 'is own and too young fer it. The vixen 'ad been killed by the 'unt. I don't like the 'unt. Live and let live. And foxes keep the rats down. Nasty things, rats. That's why me and Spot goes ratting. Lots of farmers 'ere calls us in. Better than the council ratman, Spot is. And better'n poison. Nasty stuff, poison."

Storm lay quiet as the surprisingly gentle hands soothed the ointment over the cuts.

"They're 'ealing nicely, but I wouldn't let 'im walk too far today, lad," Tom said. "I tell you what, stay in the cave, there won't be nobody about, and I'll bring you a bit of food. I got permission to catch rabbits and 'ares on the land 'ere, and there's enough of those. And there's fish in the pool beyond the canal. Farmer don't mind me fishing there. I keep 'is rats down for 'im, and and 'elps with the pigs. Not like 'aving a pig of yer own, though," he added wistfully. "Pigs is nice beasts."

"I can fish. I've got a line," Paddy Joe said.

"You catch me some fish and we'll swop it fer rabbit pie. Exchange ain't no robbery. I'm a dab 'and at pie . . . And dampers. Yer know 'ow to make dampers?"

Paddy Joe nodded.

"The pool's just round the bend, yer can't see it because o' the staircase locks. Leave your dog in my 'ut. That leg needs restin'!"

There were steps beside the locks, and Paddy Joe followed Tom down them after he had packed his rucksack again and made sure he had not left telltale traces in the cave. The morning was brightening, and a mist lay in the hollows, on which the sun dazzled. Storm stayed at heel, limping slightly, and the terrier ran ahead, her busy nose thrusting into every hole and corner, her small tail waving vigorously. She came back several times to push her muzzle into her master's hand and romped off gaily.

Tom's hut was bigger than Paddy Joe had expected, and surprisingly neat and clean. There was a tiny corner behind it planted with flowers, and a climbing rose grew over the door. Inside everything was swept and scrubbed; the camp bed was covered in a bright blanket, and a shelf held groceries and pans, while beneath it was a Calor gas cooker with two rings and a grill.

"I were in the Navy during the war," Tom said. "I like everything shipshape. You let yer dog lie here, quiet, and he'll not be tempted to run on that leg of his. Do him good to rest it. He'll be OK here. Nobody ever comes to my little 'ut."

Storm watched anxiously as Paddy Joe foraged in his rucksack for his fishing tackle. He had been told to stay, and stay he would, but he did not like being left behind. His eyes watched the door as it closed, and Paddy Joe, looking in through the window, saw the dog's head turn and Storm looked at him reproachfully.

It was lonely without his dog. Tom went off with his scythe to finish the weed-cutting along the towpath. The gentle putt putt of a boat sounded in the distance, and Paddy Joe hurried over to the pool. He had barely time to drop down out of sight when the boat arrived in the lock, and he heard Tom greet the boatmen, who were obviously well known to him. There was an exchange of jokes, and a bark from Spot, and then the sound of water rushing out of the locks into the reach below.

Paddy Joe took his knife and dug in the soft earth, hunting for worms. He found four. The sun was already strong, and day well begun. He looked at the pool. There was an overhang where the water was deep, and there might be perch there. He dropped his baited hook, and sat drowsily, thinking of nothing. A Painted Lady butterfly fluttered above the willowherb that was already going to seed. A few leaves drifted from the tree above his head. A dipper preened its feathers on the bough of a tree which grew out of the bank opposite, and hung close to the water. A head parted the reeds on the far side of the pool, and Paddy Joe found himself looking at a piebald pony which gazed at him, fascinated. He hoped it would stay away, as if it came over to him there would be little chance of fish. A heron brooded like a statue in the distant shallows.

There was a gentle tug on the line, a nibble of interest. Paddy Joe held his breath as it came again, and he tried to remember everything that Tomkin had taught him. Strike sharply. Don't hesitate, or you'll lose the fish. He struck, and a moment later the tug on the line and the flurry on the water told him that his fish was truly hooked. He began to wind in the line, but this was a fighter, not giving in easily, and once it leaped out of the water, and tried to run across the pool. Paddy Joe wound his line on to the handreel, holding it firm. It was not as easy as fishing with a rod and reel, but he did not care. If he could only catch a few fish he would not feel so mean about taking food from Tom Vence, who

76

was obviously far from being well off. He heard Tom's ready laugh and an answering guffaw from the lock, and Spot barked. He pulled in his fish, a nice little perch that must have weighed just over a pound, and killed it. It had been well and truly hooked.

The voices died away in the distance. A cow lowed near by. The piebald horse moved away from the pool and began to graze. Spot ran to Paddy Joe, sniffed at the fish and ran back again. The sound of the boat engine was now distant, and Tom Vence waved to Paddy Joe from the canal bank and put his thumb up in an "all's well" gesture.

By lunchtime Paddy Joe had four perch, and he took them proudly to Tom, who whistled when he saw them.

"There's plenty for both of us," he said. "Nothing like a nice perch, though some say it tastes muddy. We'll 'ave some taters with it. Farmer gives me those. And what about pancakes fer afters? I never knew a lad as didn't like pancakes."

Storm greeted Paddy Joe extravagantly, jumping up to lick his face. Tom bent to look at the cut on the dog's leg.

" 'Ealing nicely," he said, " 'e'll be able to walk on that without trouble termorrow."

"I can sleep in the cave again and he need not walk until tomorrow," Paddy Joe said. Vence looked at him thoughtfully.

"No one knows that cave, not even the lads. Surprised me that yer found it. It's well 'idden."

"It looked like cave country," Paddy Joe said. "I've a friend who showed me how to look. He says you look at the land and the way it slopes and the kind of rocks, and the waterfalls, and then hunt about. He was a commando in the war."

"A useful lad," Tom observed. He had peeled potatoes and gutted the perch, his hands clever and careful and unbelievably deft. "I likes cookin'. That's why I makes rabbit pie. Nothing like a bit when yer sharpset, and it's easy fer lunch. I shoots the rabbits at dusk. Got a nice little gun and got me licence fer it. Don't do to go agin the law these days. Not like the old days. You got ter keep on the right side of the perlice or yer'll end up doin' a stretch and I couldn't stand bein' in jug. Shut in, not like 'ere. I lived outside all me life. Only two winters ago, I was in the 'ospital wiv pleurisy so farmer let me 'ave this 'ut, and I moved it down to the edge of 'is land so I'd be on me own, and not 'ave close neighbours. Seemed funny at first, but I got to like 'avin' me own bits and pieces. 'is cowman's missus gave me the blanket and the rug, and them pictures of 'orses. I like 'eavy 'orses. Used ter work wiv a team of Shires, and get 'em up for shows. Spend all night polishin' the 'arness and rubbin' brilliantine on their coats to make 'em shine, and braidin' their manes and tails, and doin' the feather on their legs wi' bran. There's not many can do a big 'orse now, I can tell yer."

"What colour were they?" Paddy Joe asked. The smell of the frying fish was making him hungry.

Tom put the fish on a plate and turned the grill low to keep them warm. He wiped the frying pan out with newspaper and poured in the batter. Paddy Joe remembered the guinea fowl eggs, and produced them from his rucksack.

"That's useful," Tom said approvingly. He put the eggs in an empty baked bean tin that he had cleaned out and kept on the shelf. "Big black and white 'orses wiv white socks. Lovely creatures, they was. One was called Jet and one was Emperor and a mare called Queenie. Gentle as a baby and she had twelve lovely foals in the years I knew 'er. She'd mother 'em all and any orphans that came along. I missed that mare when she died. Used ter sleep beside 'er in the straw. Nothin' like the smell of 'orses. It were a bad day when they invented the motor car. A lorry ain't like a 'orse. I never took to drivin'. So I 'ad to give up, because farmer got a tractor. Done a lot of things in me time. But I couldn't master machinery. 'orrible noisy smelly things, tractors."

Tom brought out the perch and put them on two tin plates. He added the potatoes, and found two battered forks. For a few minutes there was no sound but that of the pigeons crooning in the trees and the water splashing from the lock gate, and the surge of the waterfall on the hill behind them. Far away, cars raced past on the road. A swan drifted slowly towards them, eyeing their plates. Tom laughed and went inside the hut and came out again with a couple of slices of bread which he threw to the bird.

"Old scrounger, that old cob," he said. "'Is mate died two years ago and 'e's never found another. Mate fer life, swans do. 'E's lonely, poor old boy. Comes up 'ere every day."

The swan ate the bread greedily, and sailed away again, and Spot ran down the bank to watch him. She came back to sit beside her master and eye every mouthful that he took until he laughed and tossed her a piece of perch.

"Nothin' like fresh air to sharpen yer appetite," Tom said, when Paddy Joe had eaten three pancakes and was sure he could eat no more. He felt sleepy and at ease for the first time for days, though there was a tiny warning niggle inside his head.

"Yer can wash up in the spring," Tom said. "And that's fer drinking too. Comes out of the 'ill just before the waterfall and it's clean and fresh as if God 'ad made it yesterday."

Paddy Joe washed the dishes and sent Storm back to lie in the hut, warning him also to be quiet. He went back to the pool, but the sun was high and the perch were no longer feeding, and he fell asleep, lying in the dappled shadow under an alder, lost to everything until Tom shook him gently awake.

"Supper time soon," he said. "I'm going up to the shop. She stays open till eight. Nobody cares, here-abouts. I find out all the news when I goes shoppin'. Proper old gossip is Mrs Turner."

Paddy Joe and Storm crawled under a dense bush and waited. The uneasiness had returned. Suppose the woman mentioned them? Suppose Mr Throstle had offered a reward for information? Suppose the police were looking for him? Suppose something happened to Tom Vence and he got run over too, like Grandee? Time slowed to a standstill. The sun was low in the sky, and the shadows lengthened. The croon of the pigeons was a maddening noise that never ceased. You can't trust n-o—o-o-o-n-e. You can't trust n—o-o-o-on-e.

There was a low soft whistle, and Vence appeared, carrying a loaded shopping bag. "Well, lad, I 'eard gossip all right," Vence said. He looked at Paddy Joe consideringly. "I don't usually ask questions and I don't tell no tales, but I likes to know the rights of a thing. I don't like ter be in trouble. Jug's no place fer an old man and I got me dog ter think of. Spot's the only thing I got left, and she's more important ter me than anything else in the 'ole world. Anyone 'urts my Spot, and I'd 'arf kill 'im. Not sure I wouldn't quite kill 'im."

"What did you hear?" Paddy Joe asked. His heart bumped uncomfortably as he was sure he knew the answer.

"I 'eard as a boy and an Alsatian dog 'ad run away from 'ome and the police 'as asked anyone 'as saw 'em to tell 'em so. They didn't say why 'e run away. 'E might 'ave good reasons. Mrs Turner in the shop told 'em she 'ad a boy in the shop last night, and the dog looked fair vicious. And the boy acted suspicious."

"My grandmother died," Paddy Joe said. "And they want to put me in a boys' home and put Storm to sleep." It was difficult to say without a trembling lip and it was even worse to think about now. If he had to go back . . . He couldn't say anything more, and he clasped his hands tightly together, the nails digging into the palms, and waited for Vence to speak.

"And the dog's all yer got, like me and Spot," Vence said. "All right, lad. That's good enough fer me. But yer can't run fer ever. What are yer goin' to do?"

"The man I was telling you about, the commando," Paddy Joe said, when he was able to speak again. "He works for a friend of my grandmother's. Only they've gone fishing in Scotland and I don't know where. They come home next week. They'll take Storm. He can't be put to sleep. He's only three."

Storm had moved close to Paddy Joe and was looking into his face. Paddy Joe was his world, his reason for living, his most prized and cherished possession. There was no one else who mattered. He put his head on the boy's knee, and Spot moved jealously to her own master and curled up close and nuzzled his hand. Vence stroked her gently, and she licked his knuckles.

"Dogs!" Vence said. "I know just 'ow yer feel, lad. Yer can trust me. So long as yer aren't on the run fer always. A bit o' camping out never 'urt no one, but yer can't live that way fer ever, not a lad like yerself. Anyone wanted ter put Spot down, I'd put 'im down. They wanted me ter go into a 'ome fer old men, as I slept rough, but I couldn't face it. Being locked up at night and not seein' stars and free ter come and go whenever I wanted. Not bein' without me dog. The farmer 'ere knows 'ow I feel. 'e's a bit of an odd bod 'imself. And 'e's crazy about 'is beasts. Got the best beasts in the county. 'E'll 'elp yer."

Paddy Joe was still uneasy. It was horrible to think that now everyone had heard that a boy and a dog was missing, though he had known it was likely. Mr Throstle would hardly be likely to sit quietly and let him vanish altogether. But now it had happened it was worse than he imagined. He would have to keep out of sight, and keep Storm out of sight and that was not going to be easy.

"Don't worry, lad," Vence said. "I knows 'ow yer feel, and so will Johnnie Blackett. 'E's the farmer 'as let me 'ave this 'ut on 'is bit o' land. 'E'll 'elp and 'e's got a grand 'iding place that'll tide yer over for a day or two. No one'll ever think of looking where 'e can 'ide yer, and I only got ter tell 'im why yer running, and 'e'll understand yer got ter run."

"It's only for another week," Paddy Joe said.

Vence nodded.

"I 'ad a calendar once," he said unexpectedly. "It 'ad a picture of a dog on it. And underneath it said,

'Brothers and sisters I bid yer beware
Of givin' yer 'eart ter a dog ter tear.'

"There's never bin anything truer written, but nobody 'oo 'adn't 'ad a dog would ever understand. Cheer up, lad, world ain't ended yet. We'll get yer out of it some'ow . . ."

"Are they looking for me?" Paddy Joe asked.

"Mrs Turner wouldn't never keep 'er mouth shut. Fair wicked old busybody she is too," Vence said. "They were asking fer anyone as'd given yer a lift ter get in touch, but when I was in the shop Mrs Turner was 'avin' second thoughts and was goin' ter tell 'em as she 'adn't 'eard a car, and she thought yer were on foot after all, and might still be 'idin' 'ere. Luckily they don't know the cave. They 'aven't begun to look along the

82

canal yet, and they 'aven't got dogs. I'm not sure that they really believe 'er at present, but we better not take chances. She asked me if I'd seen yer and I said nobody 'ad passed me 'ut today, which is true as yer 'aven't passed it! I'll show yer the way to the farmhouse. Johnnie lives alone. Never 'ad time to wed. I'll tell 'im, and 'e'll help, but yer best get away from 'ere. It won't be safe once they start really lookin' and that dog 'as left marks of 'is big feet all over the place. Unmistakable those are. Only 'ope they 'aven't got sharp eyes. Not everyone can read a trail."

There was the note of a car drawing up on the road beyond the wall, and a voice sounded, far too close.

"It may be nothing but we'll not take chances," Vence said, and picked up his bag and signalled to Paddy Joe, who hoisted his rucksack over his shoulders, beckoning to Storm. A moment later, they had melted into the trees. Tom Vence for all his size, vanished in the shadows, and proved as delicate on his feet as Tomkin. They were silent ghosts, running through the woodlands; they were refugees, racing away from an erupting volcano; they were hunters seeking deer. They were a man and a boy, evading capture, and Paddy Joe was desperately afraid.

Chapter Seven

Paddy Joe climbed behind Tom Vence, his thoughts seething through his head. He wished he could stop thinking, but it was impossible. He had always had a busy brain and a great deal of imagination. He tried to concentrate on keeping quiet, but they reached the top of the little cliff and walked into a narrow lane, where he had nothing to do but follow Tom and now his thoughts took charge.

It was easy enough to run away. It was not so easy to stay away, and Paddy Joe suddenly began to wonder what would happen if he were found before the colonel came home. He was afraid that everyone would be furious with him. Certainly Mr Throstle would be very angry indeed, and Mr Throstle was frightening enough when he was not angry. It was very difficult to believe that the solicitor had ever been young himself. He seemed to have no understanding at all of a boy's viewpoint. Paddy Joe had always been afraid of the man, of his brusque manner, and unnerving habit of clearing his throat loudly and saying in a sharp voice, "Well, Patrick, and what have you been up to this time?" as if Paddy Joe was always in mischief, which certainly wasn't true.

At least, not completely true. There had been the broken greenhouse window, and the time that he and Storm were marooned on an island in the river when they tried to cross by a raft and the raft sank under them. There had been a sudden rainstorm in the hills, and the river had run fast and unnervingly deep, water coming down in a peaty spate that took them by surprise. Luckily the man at the farm had seen them, and had borrowed a boat. Grandee had been angry that time and Tomkin had been furious.

"After all I've told you," he said. "Think before you act, Paddy Joe, or you'll never live to see your grandchildren. Never have any, for that matter."

That had been frightening. Paddy Joe had never trusted water since. You never knew what it would do. He had learned not to trust the tides either, after almost being cut off on a rocky beach with a cliff behind him. No one had ever known about that.

It was far from comforting to remember other escapades now that he was engaged on the most desperate one of all. Suppose he had begged Mr Throstle to put Storm in kennels till the colonel came home? But that would not have worked. No one ever made Mr Throstle change his mind, and he hated dogs. Grandee thought he had been bitten by one, perhaps long ago, and he had never forgotten. Whenever he came to see her he told her how stupid she was to buy an Alsatian and an Alsatian that had been abused in his puppy days, and was likely to be totally untrustworthy. He told her of others of the breed he had known and how unreliable they were. But Grandee in her own way had been as obstinate as the solicitor, and Paddy Joe had inherited her obstinacy. He had made up his mind, and it was no use turning back. Tomkin had taught him all kinds of ways of stalking and hiding, and he would make use of them.

Tom Vence was walking ahead of him, and Spot was a glimmer of white in the faint shine of a new moon. Eyes adjusted to darkness and Paddy Joe could see quite well. There were trees here, but he knew that not so far ahead the wide moors stretched towards the town, and there would be little cover there. It was a worrying thought. He was used to woodland, and had never tried to hide on open ground before.

There were lights far below, as torches shone on the ground. Vence gripped Paddy Joe's shoulder, and Paddy Joe jumped.

"Your dog's pawmarks are unmistakable. But they haven't got dogs with them. And it might not be the police anyway. There's a chance yet. I'll 'ave to think. Sure yer don't want to go back to 'em? Might be easier in the long run, lad."

"No," Paddy Joe said. "Mr Throstle'll be so mad with me he'll put Storm to sleep at once. He hates dogs. I think he hates boys too."

"Fair enough," Vence said. "I'll sort summat out. This way, lad."

They skirted the edge of a field high with barley, taking care not to tread in the growing cereal. It was not easy walking, as there were furrows round the head-lands, and a steep ditch that sloped suddenly in places where the bank had fallen away. There had been so much rain recently that parts of the crop were flattened, and the ground was completely sodden.

The high hedge protected them from a wind that was growing to gale force, sounding noisily in their ears. The terrier ran on but Storm kept at heel, guarding Paddy Joe, his ears alert, uneasy because of the wind noise that masked other noises, and aware of human voices far behind. Paddy Joe was sure that men were searching for signs of him. It was a terrifying conviction.

He vowed that never in his life would he hunt any animal. It was frightening to think that he was the quarry. He did not want to be caught, and he was only at the beginning of his adventure. His heart thumped uncomfortably and he began to feel sick. Tom Vence guessed his feelings, but there was little he could do to help. He felt sorry for the lad, alone in the world, and afraid that his dog would be killed if he were caught. People weren't much use, Tom thought. He had never had time for people himself; they weren't reliable and many of them failed to trust Tom, thinking maybe he'd make off with a purse, or do them a mischief. They did not know that Tom was honest according to his lights, and might once have lifted a hare he didn't ought to 'ave touched, but he'd never cheat a man of his own money. Never steal anything from anyone, Tom wouldn't. It was wrong, anyway you looked at it. Property was property. But who could prove that a running hare belonged to him? It belonged to God. Tom believed in God wholeheartedly and trusted his God, and he knew that if he did so all would go well with the lad and his dog. Patrick Joseph Rafferty, his name was. They'd said so on the radio. Mrs Turner had heard the news item and remembered it in detail, trust her, the old besom. Vence had no time at all for her.

Paddy Joe they called him. A nice lad, and he deserved helping. Vence gripped Paddy Joe's arm reassuringly.

"It'll be OK lad, yer'll see," he said, and Paddy Joe felt a sudden surge of confidence. Vence was the same kind of man as Tomkin, in his own way, and Tomkin was total safety, always reliable, always knowing the right thing to do.

"Nip into the barn, while I go and see Johnnie," Vence whispered, and Paddy Joe crept through the door, which was ajar, and found himself in straw-lined darkness. A hen cackled and a dog barked, and Vence shouted cheerily.

"Hey, Johnnie. It's me."

"You old rogue," a voice said, and a door shut and Paddy Joe was left alone, sitting on the scattered straw, while Storm pressed against him. There was a sudden scurry and an odd noise. Paddy Joe jumped and Storm growled, and a half-grown cat swore vigorously and ran for the door. Paddy Joe's foot warned Storm and the dog lay still, knowing he must not make a sound, sensing that the two of them had to be hidden, remain unseen and unheard, and aware, from Paddy Joe's tenseness, that this was vitally important. The two of them might have been statues, except for their slow breathing. The straw was dusty and irritated the boy's nostrils. He longed to sneeze, and pressed his hand hard against his lip, under his nose, as Tomkin had shown him. The urge vanished, and there was no sound except a faint uncanny snoring above his head. He looked up, and saw enormous saucer eyes staring at him, and knew that an owl nested in the rafters. He prayed that it would stay there and not think he was a threat to its safety. All he needed was to be divebombed by a furious owl. He needed it like he needed a hole in the head, as his American friend Hank used to say at school.

The minutes seemed endless. Time might have stopped. Paddy Joe listened and heard a sheep bleat in a field nearby, and the rustle of chickens moving in the henhouse that they had passed as they entered the yard. There was a scamper, a scurry and a squeak, and the cat caught a mouse. Storm's ears pricked alertly. The owl snored again. What was Tom Vence doing? Supposing he had betrayed them and was phoning the police to tell them to come here and search the barn? Supposing Mr Throstle had offered a big reward for his capture? But that was too silly. Paddy Joe began to count, to keep his thoughts from wandering and to ensure that he did not terrify himself even further. It was so easy to think up frightening ideas, and make matters seem even worse than they were. And he has hungry again. They had not stopped for supper. He found bread and cheese, feeling in the dark in his rucksack. Storm was hungry enough to eat bread too, and Paddy Joe counted the mouthfuls and counted the number of times he chewed each piece. One. Two . . . six . . . ten . . . Where was Tom Vence? Suppose he had just gone away and left them in the barn? They'd be found in the morning, as sure as lambs grew into sheep. Suppose he'd forgotten why they'd come? He was old, maybe older than Martha, and old people often forget. Even Grandee sometimes forgot things. Suppose something had happened, and Tom's friend wasn't going to help. Why should he?

It was miserable sitting there in the dark. It would be better to pretend he was someone else, and not Paddy Joe at all. He was a spy waiting for a rendezvous. He had an urgent message to collect, and the forthcoming battle depended on him. He knew where the troops were deployed, but there was still one outpost that he had missed, and the man meeting him was bringing news of it. His dog was his messenger, and when the man came he would fix the vital paper to Storm's collar, and the Alsatian would carry it through the trenches, running swift and silent as a wolf on the trail. Paddy Joe was so engrossed in his daydream that when Tom Vence spoke softly from the doorway he jumped uncontrollably and Storm, startled, growled.

"It's all right, lad. Come on out."

Paddy Joe stood up and followed Vence across the yard and into the farmhouse kitchen. The bright light made him blink. The farmer, a young man dressed in breeches and an open-necked shirt, grinned at him.

"Tom came to the right man," he said lazily. "Any other age, I'd have been a smuggler or a highwayman, anything for a dare and some adventure. Nothing left to do now except farm my land and wish something exciting'd happen. It never does. But I bet life's a bit too exciting for you just now, eh, lad?"

He was an enormous man with a booming voice and a dark beard that hid half his face. Paddy Joe could imagine him swaggering on a quarter deck with the skull and crossbones flying above his head and a motley crew jumping at his commands, terrified to disobey him. He could imagine him riding out at night, yelling at the coachman to stand and deliver, or galloping across a prairie, firing at Indians, or beating every man to the draw in a shooting match.

"No one'll look for you here tonight," the man said. "They might come, but this is an old place, built in the days when you could be hanged or burnt for being a Roman Catholic. My folk always did stick to the most unpopular cause, so there's a priest-hole and you can slip inside with your dog. By the time I've sprayed the place against moth and flies . . . awful plague of the things this year—no one'll be able to smell anything. Even if they bring dogs, but they won't come here."

"You'll be safe with Johnnie," Tom said. "And I'll be getting back. They might come looking for me. And want to know where I bin."

"That one's easy enough to answer," Johnnie said. "I went rabbiting tonight. The little beasts are coming back all over the farm, and what's more, they don't burrow any more. They live on top like the hares. I bagged three. Take this fellow, and they'll not ask you anything else."

Vence grinned.

"They might ask 'ow I shot me a rabbit without me gun," he said, and Johnnie roared with laughter and handed over his spare shotgun and some shot. "Bring it back tomorrow," he said. "I'll let you know what happened to our refugee here when you come."

Tom stowed the rabbit in the enormous pocket of his coat, and winked at Paddy Joe.

"You've done me a good turn already, lad," he said. "Got me a rabbit without the bother of 'untin' meself. Good luck, then. Yer can write and tell Johnnie what 'appened when yer meets yer folk, and Johnnie'll tell me. Rough End Farm, Pangley. Everyone knows Johnnie Blackett round 'ere. I'd like ter know yer got it all sorted right."

He went, and Paddy Joe was sorry to see him go.

"We'll get warning from the dogs if anyone comes," Johnnie said. "Hungry, boy?" He laughed again. "And that's a damn silly question to ask any growing lad. Come on, eat up. I was just going to start my meal."

He went to the pantry and found a meaty bone for Storm, and took another from the deep-freeze, and put it by the stove to thaw.

"My dog can wait," he said.

Paddy Joe's mouth was watering. There was a huge piece of cold roast beef on the table, and pickled onions and red cabbage, as well as a bowl of fresh fruit, a round cheese, and a crusty loaf of bread.

"I always pick a cowman with a wife who's a damn good cook," Johnnie said. "I was born greedy. I've never found a woman good enough to work on a farm though. You need a special sort of wife if you're a man like me. I forget everything when I'm busy with the beasts. They come first. No use having beasts if you don't give all your time to them . . . I've got the best herd in the county, and three first-prize winners, and a champion bull, and none of that happened by accident."

Paddy Joe was too busy eating roast beef and pickles to do more than nod. Johnnie could eat and talk at the same time, and he obviously enjoyed talking. He was telling Paddy Joe about his high milking yields when his dog barked, outside.

"Into the priest-hole," Johnnie said. He slapped his thigh. "By gum, I'm enjoying this. You've made a dull week interesting. I never thought we'd use this again, for real."

He pressed a small knothole in the wall and a cupboard door slid open to expose a gap in the back of it big enough to allow Paddy Joe and Storm to slip inside. There was a light shining, and a camp bed, a chair, a table, and a rug were revealed by it. Johnnie put down meat for the dog, and gave Paddy Joe his plate and cup and saucer.

"Not a word," he said urgently, and shut the door. There was not even a crack to show the light. Paddy Joe went on eating and Storm finished the meat and lay down, obedient to the urgent sign for silence.

The wall of the priest-hole was stone, and Paddy Joe could see now that the farmhouse was very old. He wondered if there were ghosts, and he sniffed uneasily at an odd smell that percolated through to him, and then realised that it must be the moth spray that Johnnie had mentioned. It would cover every other smell.

There was a knock on the outer door, which echoed inside the priest-hole. Johnnie heard voices, but did not hear what they said. He was sleepy, and lay on the bed, his hand stroking Storm's ears. He wondered who had sheltered there in the past, what kind of men had hidden, and what fears had dominated them. Fear of capture always, but also fear of death, of hanging or burning at the stake, of the torture chamber. Men who had run from Elizabeth when Drake roamed the high seas, men who had hidden from Cromwell, when Roundheads stormed across England and many men were afraid. Men who had lain as he lay now and heard muffled voices in the kitchen. Paddy Joe forced himself to think of the kitchen as it must have been then, no longer lit by electricity, but lit by candles, or oil lamps, with a wood stove for cooking, and old oak chairs and tables. Suppose the men who had come now knew of the priest-hole?

But nothing happened. The voices died away. Paddy

Joe looked at his watch. He had forgotten to wind it, and it had stopped. He felt bereft, not knowing the time. He dozed, and dreamed of men who chased him while he ran and ran and his pulses raced, and the ground beneath him gave way and he was falling, falling . . . He woke with a horrible jump and a thumping heart as the door slid open.

"All clear, son," Johnnie said. "It was only my cowman about a sick beast. But you'd best stay there, in case Sam sees you in the morning. He's a newcomer and knows nothing about the priest-hole. He'll be here about four-thirty and it's after midnight now. When he's finished milking he'll be down in the far field and I'll drive you to town. You can't stay here. It's too close to the village where you were seen. You want to go farther on. You're not scared, shut in here?"

Paddy Joe shook his head. Johnnie turned off the light.

"The switch is by the door, and that little room off the back there's a bathroom. All mod. con, even in a priest-hole. It was fitted out long ago and my dad brought it up to date. He had it opened up and used it as an extra bedroom, but it intrigued me and it seemed a pity to have a disused priest-hole so I made it work again. I fixed the light so that it went on when the door shut. I thought we might open up as a showhouse if ever the farm went down the drain as it might well these days. But it's fun to have a secret nobody else knows and I'm romantic. Like the man I saw on TV the other day. He wanted a castle and bought one on an island, and is doing it up to live in. There's not much romance about these days. Sleep tight, lad, and don't worry. It'll work out. Things always do."

Paddy Joe wasn't sure of that, but he was too tired to care. His life had become so strange that he felt he would soon take almost anything for granted. It was pleasant to know so many people were willing to help him. If he made sure he kept to people who owned animals themselves he might be all right, he thought, just before sleep claimed him. There was something reassuring about all real animal people. They knew things that those who had never lived with any kind of beast would never know. This time he slept peacefully, and dreamed of nothing at all.

Chapter Eight

"You've picked a bad time for camping out," Johnnie said next day, as he drove his battered Land Rover towards the town. "It's getting cooler, and we're in for a succession of storms. You can tell from the sky, and the feel of the air, and the way the beasts behave. There's nasty weather ahead."

It was unpleasant hearing. It would be difficult to keep his clothes dry if there were frequent thunder showers, and he hated Storm getting wet through. The dog had had one or two severe chills in his time, which had affected his kidneys, and Paddy Joe did not want to have to take him to the vet again. But if the dog became ill he would have no choice, even if it meant giving up his effort to stay free until the colonel came home on August the twelfth. Paddy Joe had left home on the second and this was the third day of his escapade. It must be the fifth of August, which meant there was still a whole week to get through. Paddy Joe sighed.

Johnnie said nothing. He was wondering if perhaps the kindest thing he could do was to hand the boy over to the authorities. The mood of the night before had been sobered by dawn. Johnnie often had second thoughts. There was a police station in the town. He felt grim and uneasy. Tom Vence had a persuasive tongue. Surely no man could really intend to have the dog put down. But the dog would constitute a problem if the boy was going into a children's home. And Alsatians cost a lot of money to feed. He could not offer the dog a home. Neither could he cold-bloodedly turn the boy over to the authorities. That would leave him feeling a heel for the rest of his life. Much against his soberer judgment, Johnnie was going to go along with the adventure, but he would worry now until he knew the boy had reached his friends. Johnnie wished there was something more he could do, but there was not. It was impossible to hide the boy and the dog in the priest-hole indefinitely and Sam Trent, his cowman, was both observant and curious. And so was his wife, who cleaned the house for Johnnie. It wasn't possible to keep either of them out of the way for a whole week. The Trents would be suspicious, as he could not hope to hide all trace of visitors and Storm would have to be let out regularly for exercise. He was too big to keep out of sight. It was impossible to keep Sam away from the yard, or tell his wife not to clean the house. Johnnie had never done such a thing before.

Johnnie tried to remember back to the year that he was twelve. At the time they had owned a very bad-tempered bull, and his father had been gored. Johnnie suddenly remembered lying awake in the night, sure his father would die, and the terrifying feeling of desolation that had come over him. His mother had gone to the hospital and left him alone on the farm, with only a simple-minded and unreliable cowman for company.

"You'll have to cope alone, Johnnie," she said. "I'm relying on you. I'm not leaving your dad, not till I know, one way or the other."

The vet shot the bull. They had managed to pen it, but no one could get near it. It lay in the farmyard and Johnnie had to cope with the knacker who came to take it away because the man . . . what was his name, Billy . . . Billy had been frightened of the knacker, and gone off, out of sight. Billy was frightened of most things and most people, and Johnnie soon realised that everything now depended on him. He had supervised the milking and ensured that the churns were ready for the lorry. He had mucked out, and had prepared the feed-stuffs and looked after the cattle, the hens and the pigs, and felt half-sick with responsibility and completely exhausted.

His mother had come home, but it had been nearly two weeks before they knew whether his father would live or die, and in that time Johnnie had grown up and had taken over, because his mother was so distracted that she could do nothing right. She would start to get a meal, and then forget what she had started, and Johnnie would find her standing staring out into the yard, looking at the bull's empty pen. He cooked for both of them, and shopped, and fetched and carried. His father began to get better, and came home at the end of six weeks.

"We don't know what we'd have done without you, son," he said, looking round the place, which was as well cared for as was possible for any twelve year old left on his own, and Johnnie had walked with pride for days, so pleased at having succeeded in something so difficult. He had even called the vet for a coughing cow, and the sow had farrowed and they had not lost a single one of the litter. Johnnie had stood beside her, ensuring that she did not lie on any of them, moving them away from her as soon as they were born.

Paddy Joe was the same age as Johnnie had been then. Whatever happened, Paddy Joe had made his own mind up, for good or ill. It was up to him, and not to Johnnie. The farmer decided not to interfere.

"You'll need to keep your eyes open and find shelter," he said, looking at the sky. "Those clouds are thunderheads." Paddy Joe looked up at the huge black anvil shaped clouds towering above them. The morning had started fine, but soon clouded over. Johnnie drove the Land-Rover into a lay-by.

"There's about an hour before it breaks, I reckon," he said. He looked at Paddy Joe, frowning, "Look, son, I'm not happy about you. I wish you could stay with me, but it's too risky. I'm going to make you a loan. You can send the money back as soon as you meet your friends."

"I don't need money," Paddy Joe said.

"Rubbish. If you can buy enough food to keep you going you've a better chance of keeping out of sight. How much longer have you got to manage?"

"Till the twelfth," Paddy Joe said miserably. It seemed a lifetime away.

"If you get stuck, that's my phone number," Johnnie said, scribbling the number on the torn-off top of a bill. "Ring me and I'll try and work something out. I can't let you go off without knowing you can get in touch. I wish you'd give up, though, son. It might be better."

Paddy Joe shook his head.

"They'll put Storm to sleep," he said. "They mean it. And I don't want to go into the Home till I know he's safe."

There was nothing more to say.

Johnnie pushed down the clutch, put the Land-Rover into gear, and started off, thrusting out his hand as he did so. There were three pound notes in it. He dropped them, and accelerated. Paddy Joe picked the money up. He hadn't wanted to take it, but Johnnie had left him no choice. He tucked the money safely away, and watched the Land-Rover dwindle in the distance. It was only a short walk to the town. Johnnie had not wanted to risk them being seen and had dropped him before they reached houses, first making sure that no one else was near. It would not be wise to walk on the road. A boy and an Alsatian dog would be too conspicuous. He climbed on to the moors, where furze bushes offered cover for Storm, and every time a car passed on the road, Paddy Joe dropped flat and waited until it had gone.

There was a narrow gully, lined with trees. This offered better protection and led in the right direction. It was less tiring walking as they did not need to take cover. The stream at the foot of the steep slope murmured over boulders, and a single ray of sunshine, piercing the clouds, glinted on the water.

Paddy Joe took off his shoes and socks, and walked in the cool shallows. It was good to cool his feet. His shoes were heavy, and walking on rough ground was tiring. Also if there was any pursuit the water would block it. They could travel for some distance this way. The rounded boulders were uncomfortable to tread on, but not as bad as flinty pebbles.

It was secluded under the trees. The wind rustled among them uncannily, and the branches swayed as if alive. There were few birds. Far away a curlew called, alone and desolate, the soft cry of a lost soul sobbing in the distance. A fish jumped in a little pool, falling back into the water with a plash that widened the ripples. Tiny waves broke against the bank.

The sunshine was gone. The clouds were darkening, and the wind was strengthening. It was lonely beside the river. Paddy Joe wished he had Johnnie or Vence for company. Nothing seemed quite so bad when he was with other people. It was the times alone that were worst and he had a vivid imagination. One day, he thought, he would be a writer and write a book about his adventures. If he pretended he were a famous author thinking up a story about himself and was not a real boy it might be easier. But that was such a confused thought that he abandoned it, and tried to think of words that would describe the wind that was beginning to roar like an injured beast among the trees, and the swaying branches that tossed against the sky, and the whip of foam gathering on the water as it was teased and ruffled by unseen forces that were nevertheless very much felt. It was time to leave the gully and climb on to the moors again. He could hear traffic driving to the town. The storm was almost on him. The sky was black and he must have shelter soon. He began to run.

Chapter Nine

Fifteen minutes later, out of breath and very hot, Paddy Joe reached the little town that lay sleepily on the edge of moors where the heather fought with the bracken, and the gorse and furze conquered all of them and blazed with a light of its own that glowed against the dulling sky. Before him was a sprawl of houses and straggled streets, the gardens climbing the hills, and then falling away steeply. Everyone seemed busy. Holidaymakers seethed in the streets, buying souvenirs; postcards and vases and jugs and brasses. Paddy Joe glanced in the shops and found their contents ugly.

The only shop that attracted him was a saddler's, which was almost on the edge of the moors, on the opposite side of the town. Saddles hung outside under the blind and the smell of warm leather reminded him of home, and of the colonel's two hunters, Thunder and Lightning, and of the pleasant steamy kitchen where he and Tomkin sat astride two stools and rubbed away, cleaning off the mud, and polishing with sticky saddle soap, till everything shone.

Paddy Joe ran his hand over one saddle. The leather was smooth to the touch, gleaming as a conker, immensely satisfying.

"You like leather, boy?"

The saddler was old, no taller than Paddy Joe, stooped and bald with a skin like polished cowhide. He had steelrimmed spectacles that slipped down his nose and warm brown eyes that laughed at Paddy Joe.

"I like polishing saddles," Paddy Joe said. It was

true. There was something satisfying in taking the dulled and muddy leather and rubbing until it gleamed with reflected light.

The sky split. A fireball flared on the moors and thunder crashed. The tortured clouds burst in a single movement and rain poured in a sudden torrent, drumming so loudly on the canvas blind that it sounded like an army marching past in full cavalcade.

"Come into the shop, boy," the saddler said. "We'll drown out here. Bring your dog inside too."

"He's mucky," Paddy Joe said, ashamed of Storm's matted coat.

"He won't hurt," the man said. Paddy Joe followed him into a tiny cave of a shop, where saddles hung from the ceiling, and rested on brackets on the walls, and stirrups dangled in bundles, and bundles of girths lay everywhere. A number of plaited leads, made of thick and shining leather, hung above the counter, together with belts which were patterned and tooled, each with an animal's head as a clasp. One clasp was a snake, a second a dog, a third was a horse.

There were piles of leather cases, of school satchels, of knapsacks and haversacks, of pouches and wallets, and a big handbag, with a patterned front, edged with braiding of coloured leather strip and more handsome than anything Paddy Joe had ever seen.

The shop smelled of leather, reminding Paddy Joe of horses, of Tomkin's leather apron that he wore to clean the saddles, and somehow too of warm evenings spent by the kitchen fire, while Tomkin talked to him of deer and of foxes and of the time that his terrier had unearthed a badger that had charged straight at Tomkin, snapped at his foot and bitten away half his shoe, leaving the sock untouched.

Storm had been prowling round the shop, sniffing. He walked behind the counter, and there was a sudden deep growl. "Here," Paddy Joe said, and the dog came at once.

"That's a good dog," the saddler said approvingly. "Come and see the cause of the trouble."

Paddy Joe went behind the counter, surprised to find it packed with stacks of hides, ready for working. Beyond them, on a canvas bed raised up from the floor, lay the biggest dog he had ever seen, a massive animal with a thick white coat and beautiful husky-like head.

"She's a Pyrenean mountain dog," the saddler said proudly. "She's the only family I've got now. My wife's dead, and I had one lad killed in the last war, and the other's married and living out in Canada. Got three little grandnippers now, and never set eyes on one of 'em. Here, Susie girl, show us your pups, then."

Susie stood up, and Paddy Joe, looking down, saw that part of what he had taken to be her fur was in fact six pups, fluffy and cuddly as toys. They stood on uncertain legs, looking about them, and, seeing a stranger, cuddled down together, faces hidden in one another's fur.

Susie nosed them and resumed her place on her bed. The saddler laughed.

"They've never seen anyone but me till now," he said. "She has a litter every year, and it's all she and I can bear to sell them. We'll keep these for a few weeks yet, till they are clean and biddable, and then I've owners waiting for them. She's the best mother in the world."

Susie's tail wagged acknowledgement.

"Better stay here till the rain's eased," the saddler said. By now it was drumming on the pavements, dancing in little ripples and whorls, streaming along the gutters, surging over waste paper flung down by careless hands, choking at the drains which could not carry it away.

"We'll have some tea."

The saddler put a battered kettle on a gas ring, and found a half-empty bottle of milk, and a paper bag . . . Inside the bag were four doughnuts.

"Something said to me today, buy four, you may have a visitor," the old man said. He laughed. "That's not as clever as it sounds, as my horoscope said I'd have an unexpected visitor. I'm Scorpio, the sign of the scorpion, born in November. Susie's Taurus, the bull. The day she had her pups her horoscope said that she would have a bonus that day, and if six pups isn't a bonus I'd like to know what is. Eh, boy? When's your birthday?"

"July 23rd," Paddy Joe said, with a sudden pang, because his birthday that year had been memorable. That was the day of the Royal Show, when High Glee won the Best in Show and Grandee had promised he might one day have his own horse, if their ship came home safely. Once he had thought there really was a ship at sea, bringing home a fortune, but now he knew it had just been one of Grandee's many sayings, meaning very little but that if there was enough money, then his own horse might be a possibility.

"You're Leo," the saddler said, with the air of someone making a great discovery. He dived under the counter and reappeared with a creased and grimy newspaper.

"Your horoscope for today says 'Be wary of strangers. Good fortune will come your way, but you must take care. If you are starting a new venture, be assured of success.' Now how's that for encouragement?"

The colonel and Tomkin both laughed at horoscopes, but Paddy Joe needed reassurance and perhaps, just once, there might be something in it. After all, Susie had her bonus, and the saddler had his unexpected visitor, and one day, in the early summer, when he had glanced at his own, he had been warned of danger. That was the day he fell into the river near the weir, and Tomkin had to swim after him, as the current was so strong. Perhaps there really was something in star forecasts. Secretly Paddy Joe felt that he was being absurd, but he did, so desperately, need to believe today's.

Tea was an unusual meal, as he had to drink out of an old jug, the saddler having only one cup in the shop. The doughnuts were delicious and Paddy Joe ate the last crumb and licked his jammy fingers, while Storm and Susie each sat beside their own masters, eyes beseeching. Each was rewarded with a small piece as dogs ought not to be given tit-bits and Tomkin was furious with Paddy Joe if he fed Storm from the table.

"I won't have a dog that's a scrounger," Tomkin always said. "Don't let him be a fool."

For all that there were times when Paddy Joe did slip an odd mouthful to the dog. It was difficult to be stern when those enormous brown eyes begged so eloquently.

The church clock was striking five when the rain stopped, and Paddy Joe walked out again into a world that dripped from roof and shingle, that swilled small gullies of water down his neck from hanging shop blinds and from trees planted in the streets. Storm walked behind him. They would have to eat again soon. Food seemed to be the major item on the day's list of needs. Paddy Joe had never before realised quite how much thought went into keeping people from being hungry. No wonder Martha seemed to spend all her days shopping and cooking.

Paddy Joe ordered Storm to wait outside the supermarket, where bright lights defeated the gloom left by the rain. He wandered around, not sure what was best to buy.

He couldn't stay in the town, as he would be very

obvious there, as not belonging. Out on the moors he might find refuge, perhaps in a cave or a hut or an empty house, and remain unseen. Finally he bought a whole pound of cheese, a meat pie, and a pound of shin beef for Storm, a packet of raisins, and a bag of bread rolls. Johnnie's three pounds was very useful. He must make sure he remembered the farmer's address so that he could repay him. He wrote it on one of the paper bags. He paid for his purchases at the desk, and put them in his rucksack. His thoughts were miserable as he went out into the damp gloom of evening. Swallows were flying low, hawking across the grass of the little green outside the churchyard. That meant more rain. Paddy Joe whistled to Storm, and trudged away from the town, on to the edge of the moors that stretched in front of him for miles, unkown and bleak and secret and filled with fear.

They had only been moving for about twenty minutes when Paddy Joe heard a bark behind them. He turned, and saw the Pyrenean mountain dog from the saddler's shop. He looked towards her, puzzled, and she trotted up to him, and nudged his leg. Then, as he stood, uncertain, she ran back towards the town, and looked over her shoulder, and barked again. Storm, knowing that she wanted them to go with her, bounded after her, as fast as his sore leg allowed, and Paddy Joe had no choice but to follow.

A small needle of worry wriggled inside his mind. There must be something wrong. The saddler had said the dog never left him. He began to run. Both dogs were well ahead, and the sound of their pads on the pavement and of Paddy Joe's shoes made the few people about turn their heads and stare at them.

Paddy Joe pushed open the door of the saddler's shop. Storm raced inside, and his angry growl brought Paddy Joe to him at once. The old saddler was tied to his chair by narrow thongs of hide, and two youths were busy at the little safe which sheltered under the counter. Both cowered as Storm threatened them with bared teeth. Paddy Joe did not need to give his dog any orders now.

The old man was gagged. Paddy Joe tore off the gag, his fingers shaking. The men were no longer dangerous. Both crouched, terrified—the Pyrenean was echoing Storm's growls in a deep throaty rumble that must have been totally unnerving to the crooks.

"Get the police, son," the old man said. "Quick now. You can untie me later. There's a phone round the corner. Your dog might do as he's told, but mine got kicked and pushed out when she tried to come back in at the door and she's dying to have a bite out of those two. I can't hold her if she gets really mad. Dunno as I want to."

Paddy Joe ran. He found the call box and dialled 999. He very much wished he did not have to, as the police would want to know his name and address, and he did not want to give it. Life did get so much more complicated than you ever expected.

The squad car arrived at the shop at the same time as Paddy Joe. The policemen grinned as they saw the thieves crouched down, watching the Pyrenean mountain dog. Paddy Joe ordered Storm to sit outside the back door of the shop, and the dog slipped out swiftly, aware of urgency, although he did not know why. Paddy Joe felt that a boy alone would not rouse interest. A boy and an Alsatian were a very different matter. Susie was trembling, only too eager to reach the men and punish them for harming her and her master.

The thieves were led away, while a third policeman remained to take particulars. The saddler described how he had gone outside to empty the tea leaves from his teapot into his window boxes for fertiliser, and Susie had followed him. When he came into the shop the two men grabbed him, kicked Susie on the nose and slammed the door in her face. He was shivering with shock. The policeman made a cup of tea to help him over his fright, while Susie was petted and praised and fussed. Storm, outside the back door, was completely invisible. Paddy Joe had only to flick a finger for the Alsatian to obey. The policeman might never know the dog was there.

"Now, son, how did you happen to come back?" the policeman asked, as the saddler had told him that Paddy Joe had been in the shop that afternoon sheltering from the storm.

"Susie came after me and asked me to follow her," Paddy Joe said. He was afraid that the policeman might not believe him, but the policeman had a dog himself and knew exactly what Paddy Joe meant.

"What's your name, boy? And where do you live?"

"Pat Jones," Paddy Joe said, and, after a moment's hesitation gave the policeman the colonel's address, sure that the colonel would not mind. "I live with my uncle," he added, "only he's gone fishing and I'm doing an initiative test to see how long I can keep myself without having to ring up and ask to be rescued." He was glad he was wearing his scout beret. The policeman had not given him a second glance.

"It sounds a fine idea," the policeman said. "I hope you make it."

He went away, and the saddler rubbed his wrists wearily. The policeman had had difficulty untying the leather bootlaces that the thieves had used as thongs.

"They weren't very gentle," the old man explained. "One thing, they didn't get inside the safe. Not that it matters, as if they had they'd have had a surprise."

The old man bent down and opened the safe by twirling a small dial. Inside were needles and thread, a piece of tailor's chalk and three pairs of scissors of different sizes, as well as various small tools that Paddy Joe had never seen before.

"I never keep money here," the old man said. "But I bought the shop from someone who did, and he left the safe installed. I had a shop on the other side of town, but they pulled it down. The safe is very useful for my tools. I'd always be losing them, without it."

"If you're all right now . . ." Paddy Joe said uncertainly.

"I'm not," the old man said firmly. "I'm all shook up, and I don't want to be alone tonight. There's a spare room in my house and you showed plenty of initiative in coming back and fetching the police to me . . . So I should think it would show even more initiative to come and give me a hand and keep me company till I've got over my shock. Come along, boy. And you too, Susie. It's home time."

Paddy Joe grinned. He had somewhere to sleep that night, and another day was safely over. He helped pull down the blinds and shoot the bolts of the shop door, and then followed the old saddler across a cobbled yard where bright flowers bloomed in pots and everything was neatly stacked, and a black cat stretched on a carved wooden bench in the shelter of a white-washed wall. On the other side of the yard was a narrow lane, leading to a small house, its thatch hanging low over latticed windows which were decorated with yellow wooden shutters and window boxes full of lobelia and hanging geraniums and pelargoniums.

"I'm Solomon Hasty," the saddler said, turning his head and quite suddenly creaked noisily. Paddy Joe stared at him and realised he was laughing. "Look behind you, boy."

Paddy Joe turned round, and discovered that he was followed by a procession of animals. Storm came first, with Susie on his heels, and after them came six roly poly pups, trying desperately to keep up, and behind them, his nose high in the air as if he were trying to pretend he was on his own and not following eight dogs, was the black cat, who had just jumped down from the bench.

Paddy Joe laughed too. He was suddenly exalted, walking on feathers and breathing air richer than Jersey milk. He was safe for tonight, and had companionship, and he had just realised that being alone was even lonelier than he had thought. He needed people, and this time, someone needed him. It was wealth beyond measure, something that all the millionaires in the world could never buy.

Solomon Hasty opened his front door, and they walked into the cottage hallway, which was carpeted in red, and occupied by a yellow canary in a cage, who sang in joyous welcome. A leather-covered stool stood beside a carved table made of black oak, on which was a copper jug filled with orange flowers.

The place was crowded within seconds, but Susie walked at once to the living-room, where her own box waited her. She drove the pups inside, and went out to the kitchen. Paddy Joe was busy looking at the cottage, and it was hard to know where to start or what to look at first, it was so full of pleasures.

There were horse brasses hanging in groups above the fireplace walls, and a shelf of toby jugs, graduated from an enormous grinning one to a tiny one no bigger than Paddy Joe's thumb. The big chairs were covered in shining leather, polished to rich splendour that was only equalled by the patchwork silk cushions and the prayer rug in front of the fireplace. On the mantelpiece a china shepherdess smiled at a shepherd who carried a lamb in his arms, a china cat dressed in old-fashioned clothes danced a jig and a china monkey in even older clothes played a fiddle. Beyond them was a china Shire horse, dressed for May day, harness winking and ribbons shining and beyond him was another horse, this time made of leather, with a real saddle and girth and tiny bridle and minute stirrups.

"That one's Daydream," Solomon Hasty said, as Paddy Joe put out a finger and touched the bridle very gently. "I made him long ago, because I always wanted a horse, but I never could afford one. He's carried me miles, in my dreams. Liver and lights!" he added hurriedly, and skidded out of the room.

Paddy Joe followed him, somewhat astonished and discovered that a pan was boiling over on the gas stove and that it did indeed contain liver and lights, which obviously Susie and the black cat loved as they both were sitting watching the pan, licking their lips. Susie was eyeing Storm, but the black cat had placed himself neatly, paws together and tail tucked round them, and his green eyes saw nothing but the pan that smelled so delicious.

Paddy Joe was relieved to see that there was also a pan of onions frying, into which the old man had put some steak, and in another pan potatoes and peas cooked together, the peas in a neat little container of their own.

"Pays to economise. I like saving money," the old man said. "You lay the table, Pat. You'll find all you need in the drawer beneath the flap."

Paddy Joe found the cloth, and knives and forks and spoons. Solomon Hasty put a match to the fire, which was waiting for him to set it into life, and Storm came to see what they were doing, and returned to the kitchen again, anxious to ensure that no one forgot to feed him, with all the other animals about.

"We'll open a tin of something special, and celebrate your being here, and saving me from those men,"

Solomon Hasty said. He was delving into the back of the larder, which was stacked high with all kinds of food.

"Raspberries . . . and cream . . . and some éclairs from the freezer. I took them out to thaw yesterday. I thought they would cheer me up and now they will cheer us both up," Solomon Hasty said, and his bright eyes laughed at Paddy Joe over the top of his steel-rimmed spectacles.

Quite suddenly, Paddy Joe knew that Solomon Hasty must be a hobbit. He was small, and merry, and looked just as a hobbit ought to look. On an impulse he took the *Lord of the Rings* out of his rucksack.

"Do you know this book?" he asked.

Solomon Hasty went to the bookcase and took out another copy, only his was so well read it was falling apart. Paddy Joe needed no other answer. It was a warm thought, even if it wasn't a true one.

Later that evening he sat by the fire, while Solomon Hasty read aloud, and together they retraced their steps over familiar ground, as Solomon wanted to read again the setting out on the long journey, and the way the hobbits met Tom Bombadil. The soft well-remembered words were soothing and dreamlike, and Paddy Joe fell asleep. He woke to feel Solomon Hasty's hand on his shoulder, and it was all he could do to stay awake long enough to wash his face and hands and feet and clean his teeth. The bed he was shown to, in a little room with a sloping ceiling and roses on the wallpaper, was more comfortable than any bed he had ever known and he was asleep almost before he got into it.

He did not hear Solomon Hasty talking to the dogs, or the sound of Storm being bathed and made clean in the big kitchen, and he knew nothing again until he woke in the late morning to unfamiliar noises, and the sudden realisation that today must be Sunday and that he had found a brief sanctuary, and that both he and Storm were still safe and had remained undiscovered. The policemen had shown no curiosity. None of them had seen Storm. Perhaps no one was looking for him. Perhaps Mr Throstle was glad he had gone, and saved him a problem. Perhaps no one cared in the least.

Paddy Joe dressed himself. Storm was lying by his bed, and lifted his head and thumped his tail. His sore paw was mending, and the gash in his shoulder had been bathed again and tended. Paddy Joe sat down on the mat and put his arms round the dog's neck.

"Oh, Storm," he said. "What's to become of us?" Storm licked Paddy Joe's face.

Chapter Ten

Sunday was an island in time; Sunday was space to relax and consider; Sunday was peace. The little cottage at the back of the shop could only be reached through the shop and through the yard and down the lane. Paddy Joe sat on the bench in the garden, polishing a saddle, and imagined himself, sitting beside Tomkin, outside the colonel's stables, while inside Thunder and Lightning rustled the straw, and the air was full of the scent of warm horse.

The black cat stretched peacefully on a patch of sunshine on the cobbles. Susie lay and watched her pups roll and tease. One of them, suddenly bold, staggered towards Storm and licked the Alsatian's nose. Storm considered him with surprise, as pups were outside his experience. He put out a paw and tapped the bundle of fur, and lolled his tongue when it growled at him in annoyance. When Paddy Joe looked again the pup had curled to sleep between the Alsatian's front paws, and Storm was lying with an air of resignation on his face, plainly somewhat bewildered by his new task as puppy sitter.

Solomon Hasty was cooking. He sang softly as he worked, because Sunday was go-to-town day as far as meals were concerned. Most days were hustle-hurry days, when breakfast was a slice of toast, and lunch a ham sandwich, and supper a too-tired-to-cook meal of bacon and egg and baked beans.

But Sunday was sit-and-savour day, and breakfast had been eggs, scrambled fluffy light, and crisp golden coils of bacon, and sweet corn and black mushrooms, and fried bread, followed by toast and fresh butter and honey from a comb taken from Solomon Hasty's own hive, which stood in a corner of the yard.

Sunday dinner was cooking. Tomorrow was time enough for Paddy Joe to go on his way, Solomon Hasty said. Today they would keep each other company and enjoy conversation and he would enjoy having someone to share with, and pretend that Paddy Joe was one of the grand-nippers come over from Canada to see his old Grandad.

The smell of cooking was making Paddy Joe's mouth water. Solomon had brought a small leg of lamb, which he rubbed with garlic, and salt, and black pepper. He put an onion beneath it, to add more flavour, and added a squeeze of lemon juice. There were new potatoes, dug up that week in the potato field belonging to the farm with Shire horses that always wore Solomon's harnesses. There were peas, which Paddy Joe had podded, and baby marrows, picked from a plant whose roots grew in the tub in the corner. Its leaves made a leafy shade in which the black cat lay when the sun was too fierce.

There were raspberries, with tiny meringues that Solomon made himself, piping the shapes on to a tray, to harden in the oven. He was whipping cream and singing loudly, and the dogs and the pups were in dire trouble, as the smell made their mouths water, and their busy tongues licked continually at their lips.

When Paddy Joe came to the table he found onion sauce and mint sauce, and a thick rich gravy, and as he tasted the food, he discovered that no one else he had ever met had had any idea how food should be cooked. Nothing Martha or Tomkin made had ever tasted like this.

There was another saddle waiting to be shone after

dinner was over. He worked busily, enjoying the feel of the leather between his hands, and delighting in the rich sheen that rewarded his rubbing.

"I'll show you something, boy," Solomon Hasty said. The old man was sitting on a canvas chair, relishing the sunshine, his busy hands working on a belt of dark leather that he was marking with a sharp tool. He vanished indoors and returned with another saddle, oddly shaped, and much narrower than the saddles that Paddy Joe knew.

"It's an old cavalry saddle, over a hundred years old. The kind that they used when the Light Brigade charged at Balaclava," the saddler said. His fingers soothed the gleaming leather as if the hide was still alive. "One hundred years of polishing and shining. One hundred years of loving and caring. There's not many saddles today that will look like this one hundred years from now."

It was strange to think of men who had been dead for so long, and their hands polishing the rich leather which had the sheen and colour of a horse chestnut. Paddy Joe wondered what kind of men had used the saddle. Rich men; poor men; kind men or cruel men; men who loved their horses more than gold, or roistering gamblers, living for the toss of a dice and the satisfying feel of shining sovereigns under their hands. There was history in the saddle, and, for a moment, Paddy Joe felt a wind across his face, and saw a man in cavalry uniform spur his black charger, and ride across the sun. He turned his head sharply, but nothing moved but the shadows, teased on the pavement as the wind stroked the leaves.

He wished he could stay with Solomon Hasty for ever, but tomorrow he must leave. Solomon had work to finish, as he had promised a new bridle for the farmer's hunter, and he went into the shop, leaving

Paddy Joe with the little radio set for company.

Paddy Joe listened idly to a programme about farming, and a rather dreary mystery play and a quiz. He was more than half-asleep when he suddenly heard his own name.

"Patrick Rafferty, the boy who has been missing from his home since Thursday morning."

He switched off the set, thankful that he had been alone, and that the saddler had not heard the item. So they were busy announcing it on the news bulletins. How long did they do that for, Paddy Joe wondered. How long before they gave up, keeping him in mind, but not, any longer, of prime importance? Suppose they put his picture on television? Had they a photograph? He could not remember anything recent. There was a long ago picture of him with Storm as a pup. Grandee had no camera, and Tomkin and the colonel were not interested in that kind of photography. Both of them liked to take wildlife pictures, but neither of them took photographs of people. He had no other relatives who would want to see what he looked like. There might be an old school picture, taken at the primary school, five years ago. He had changed a lot since then.

Solomon Hasty came back, his nutcracker face smiling. It was time for tea, and Sunday was something special. Sunday supper would be special too as Solomon had visitors.

"I like cooking, boy," he said. "There's only time on Sundays, though. Smell that food?"

Paddy Joe could smell new bread and scones; there were plates of raspberries, gathered from the garden, which Solomon had put down in his deep-freeze, and thick Jersey cream. There was a sponge cake, tasting of lemon, and iced with a delicious strawberry fudge icing. Paddy Joe couldn't believe that he would have room for a meal later.

"We'll sit and read till supper time," Solomon Hasty said. "I used to think one day I'd be reading aloud to my own grandsons, like my granddad read to me. Those evenings were special, when we drew the curtains and sat by the fire, and my grandmother embroidered pillowcases, and my granddad found *David Copperfield*, or *Oliver Twist*, and read to us all. He owned the shop then, the one that was pulled down, and we lived down the road, and my da worked with him. Everyone had horses in those days; butcher and grocer and baker, parson and doctor and squire, and we were so busy making harnesses and bridles and girths there were four men in the shop too and even then the order books were always full, and the leather we got then, that was something to see. I don't know, they can't cure leather now. I remember making belts out of buckskin, soft and strong, and jesses for the falcon at the big house, and polishing till I couldn't keep my eyes open. I weren't much older than you. Fourteen I was when I started making saddles. It's all changed now."

He sighed, and began to clear away the cups and saucers and plates and Paddy Joe dried the dishes. When they returned to the living-room Solomon Hasty put the radio set on top of the cupboard.

"I can pretend you're one of my own grand-nippers," he said wistfully. "There's three of them. Tony, who's ten, and Michael, he's eight, and John, he's five. They live in Toronto. I don't suppose I'll ever see them while they're small. Maybe one day, when they're grown up, they'll come to England. Now, lad, what shall we read? *The Lord of the Rings*? I like it and you like it, eh? There's nothing quite like reading aloud, or listening to a story. It makes it a treasure to share."

Paddy Joe nodded. Susie and her pups were sprawled in front of the fireplace. Mountain dog was right, Paddy Joe thought, looking at her. She even dwarfed Storm, who was lying beside Paddy Joe's chair with his nose on the boy's shoe. Two of the pups had forsaken their mother and were curled up against the Alsatian, their small bodies startlingly white and fluffy against Storm's short black and tan coat, now beautifully clean after his bath.

It was wonderful to sit back and listen quietly. Solomon Hasty read well and his voice soothed all of them. Even Storm and Susie and the pups listened, and the black cat came in and jumped to her master's knee, and rubbed her head against the sharp corner of the book, scratching voluptuously. The animals' ears moved backwards and forwards, as if they understood every word.

The clock struck eight, and Solomon shut the book. Paddy Joe came back from a world of trolls and dragons to his own realities. It was time to feed the animals, and then to feed themselves. Animal feeding proved more demanding than he had expected as Susie had to have specially prepared meals while she was feeding the pups, and the pups had extra food too, and there were six saucers to prepare with bread soaked in bovril, and added vitamins and cod liver oil.

There was meat for Storm and meat and vegetables for Susie. Storm would never eat vegetables, and sniffed at her plate in disgust before going over to his own. Susie growled, and Solomon quieted her.

Their own meal was a cold one; a veal and ham pie, salad in a delicious dressing, and fresh peaches with cream. Soon afterwards Paddy Joe went to bed. He was setting off early in the morning. It was time to go on. He wished he could stay, but that was out of the question. Solomon knew nothing about him but he might hear the news item at any time, and once he did he might not protect the two of them, like Vence and Johnnie Blackett. Paddy Joe had been lucky so far, because both of them had helped him, but his luck could not hold for ever, and Solomon Hasty might not feel inclined to let him carry on with his adventure. He couldn't risk being found out this time. Twice was enough and he had to rely on both Vence and Johnnie keeping quiet about him. If only he could have stayed with one of them, it would have been less lonely, but it wasn't possible to keep out of sight, and neither he nor they had doubted for one minute that if found he would be dragged off home and Storm put to sleep. But suppose Mr Throstle had relented?

An image of the lawyer grew in Paddy Joe's mind; of the man's sharp nose and intense hot angry eyes; of his huge shiny shoes and his ugly hands; of his harsh crowlike voice and the way he snapped and said everything twice. Once, when Paddy Joe had been very small, the lawyer had been angry with him and lost his temper and smacked Paddy Joe hard, and told Grandee that boys needed a firm hand and no nonsense. Grandee had been very angry indeed, but the memory remained, and the knowledge too that the anger had been out of all proportion to the misdeed.

"Boys!" Paddy Joe could hear the lawyer's voice now. "Spare the rod and spoil the child and spoiling is what you're doing, ma'am. I'm telling you. I'm telling you. The boy'll grow up namby pamby, no good, useless. Pity he wasn't a girl. You could have coped with a girl. Pity."

Grandee had sent for Martha to take the child away and her voice, icy, furious, came through the door, but he had not heard her words. He had always hated the lawyer. Now he both hated and feared him. The man was so powerful and Paddy Joe himself so helpless. But Mr Throstle wasn't going to win this time. Paddy Joe was going to stay out until the twelfth. It was now the sixth. Only six more days. As soon as he could he would telephone to Tomkin and Tomkin would come for him and everything would be all right. He went to bed happier than he had been since his grandmother died. It had to be all right. Storm, lying beside the bed, was dreaming. His tail thumped and his hind leg kicked as he raced after a dream rabbit, and he gave a sudden short bark of excitement and woke himself up. He was surprised to find he was in Paddy Joe's room and not out on the moors chasing after the enticing smells that lay on the grass, and he looked at Paddy Joe sheepishly.

Paddy Joe laughed and scratched behind Storm's ear, and dropped back on to his pillow, more determined than ever that the dog must stay alive. If only he could manage it. The six days stretched ahead of him, unknown and menacing. It did not do to think. Thinking spoiled everything. The fear returned. What would the morning bring?

Chapter Eleven

Monday dawned in a flame of light, streaked by darkling cloud. Paddy Joe eyed it anxiously, knowing that more bad weather lay ahead. Solomon gave him a pack of food, and a bone for Storm, and waved goodbye as Paddy Joe turned towards the moors, which lay bleak under a sky that was darkening rapidly.

Storm raced ahead. The moorland path was excitement, rabbit scent and hare scent, rat scent and weasel scent, mouse and stoat and shrew. It was a delirium of smells, all vying with one another for attention, so that the Alsatian sped from bush to bush, put his nose down a rat hole, dug momentarily at a rabbit hole, and then sped in front of Paddy Joe and rolled friskily, kicking his legs skywards, overcome by pleasure. Tail weaving busily, he jumped up and darted ahead, to return to Paddy Joe and nose his knee and lick his hand, and once, to bark briefly at a skylark that came up suddenly almost under his nose, and soared, singing, until it was too small to see, and was nothing more than a trill of sound, carried by the wind, crying its joy to the day.

It was difficult to be downhearted. There was too much to see. A rabbit dashed away, terrified, its white scut bobbing, and Storm gave chase. The rabbit dived for cover, and fled into a burrow, where it crouched for the rest of the morning, appalled by the nearness of disaster. Storm soon forgot it, and nosed a bundle of brown feathers lying in the dust.

A second later, the partridge lost its nerve, and exploded from the ground, startling both boy and dog.

It had been shamming dead, the only defence it knew, and could not keep up the pretence while the dog stood over it. It too hid under a bush, its heart thump-thumping, and took all morning to dare the world again.

There was so much to see that Paddy Joe forgot all caution. It was not until the path led past a farm that he remembered the news bulletin. The farm was busy with chores; chink of churn and thud of milking machines; clang of pail and call of rooster. Cattle lowed and sheep bleated, and a dog barked. The bark might mean danger. Paddy Joe left the path and fought his way along a narrow sheep trail, climbing the hill.

At the top, he looked down on the farmhouse, dwarfed to unreality, at the road, along which small cars chugged like children's toys, at the patched fields and the pied moorland, and the town lying in the distance, a jumble of rooftops that spoiled the view. A blue lake glittered briefly in a few protesting rays of sunshine. Cloud streaked over the water, turning the blue to grey, killing the ripples of light. A bird chittered urgently. Paddy Joe put out his hand to take Storm's collar, and together they watched a small pointed muzzle lift from the ground, and saw the slide and the slip as the weasel hurried on, anxious to avoid encountering them. Behind it came three half-grown kits, busy and curious, rooting under stone and bush, hunting for food.

Paddy Joe found shelter behind a furze bush, in a hollow protected from the wind, and opened the pack that Solomon had given him. He thought there must be enough food for an army. He still had the cheese and rolls and butter, although the bread was very stale. He kept it. They might be glad of it later.

Inside the pack he found bacon sandwiches and hard boiled eggs and a small parcel labelled Riff. Paddy Joe had forgotten that to Solomon he had been Pat Jones and his dog Riff. He hoped that the saddler would never associate them with Patrick Joseph Rafferty, missing from his home with his dog Storm. The parcel contained chopped cooked liver and lights. It looked unappetising, but Storm did not find it so and ate eagerly. There were sandwiches for lunch, and a meat pasty; a slice of almond cake, and two apples and two bananas. Underneath was another pack, solid and hard, wrapped in foil.

Paddy Joe opened it. It contained one of the plaited leather leads, and a belt that Solomon Hasty had made the day before. He must have sat up in the night to finish it. The leather gleamed between Paddy Joe's fingers. There was a little note with it.

"Good luck, boy. Don't forget Solomon Hasty. He won't forget you, or what you did for him. Come and see me if ever you come back this way."

Paddy Joe put the note in his pocket. He fastened the lead to Storm's collar, and fitted the belt round his waist, clasping the dog's-head buckle over its hook. It was a splendid belt. He had never had one like it, and it had been made so that it would fit him even when he was grown up. Paddy Joe made a vow. When he was safe again he would write to Solomon Hasty and thank him, and perhaps his letter would help the old man to forget his loneliness for a while.

Storm growled softly. A man was walking near them. They were hidden by the bush. Paddy Joe hushed the dog and lay quiet, his hand over Storm's mouth. He could hear his own heart thumping. He did not want to be seen, in case the man had heard the news bulletin. How did the police search? Would they hunt for him for days, wondering if harm had come to him, or would they guess he had run away, and was hiding? He had only been away for four days, and there were still six more to fill before the colonel came home. He could never do it. Paddy Joe stared at an ant that was walking over his shoe, but did not see it. His thoughts were much too bleak.

When the man had gone Paddy Joe and Storm made their way along the hill top. A river ran below them, in a hidden wooded valley. The moors were bisected by little ravines where trees and bushes grew densely. They could hear the chuckle and call of the water. If they reached the river, he might be able to fish again and they would have something for supper.

The narrow hard-packed trail slipped through the heather. At times bracken grew high enough to hide them completely, and Paddy Joe practised his wood-craft. He took care to place his feet gently, never crackling a leaf, or breaking a twig, and watched that his shadow did not betray him by spreading out across the path when anyone was near. Luckily the hikers and ramblers were never quiet. All the world seemed to be on holiday this August and exploring the hills. He could hear their feet thumping over the ground and the sound of their noisy voices long before they reached him, and Storm heard the more silent walkers and gave quick warning.

There was always time to drop into the heather, and lie as quiet as a sleeping adder, until the noise had died away. No one on the hillside caught a glimpse of Paddy Joe or Storm, or knew that two pairs of eyes watched from the bushes where boy and dog lurked unseen.

Paddy Joe was thirsty by the time they reached the river. This was new territory, quite unlike the river near his home. The water seethed gently over limestone rocks that were channelled into steps, and in places were potholed, so that the deep pools were hidden treachery, into which a child might slip and vanish for ever. Paddy Joe walked under over-arching trees that hid the day, and found himself a small cove where he could fish in peace.

He used his knife to dig the earth for worms, and baited his hook. Farther down the river a fish jumped, and was still again, but ripples widened where it had leaped, until they broke against the bank in small flurries of foam. It was some time before the dancing water stilled.

Paddy Joe caught two trout in less than an hour. It was time to vanish, as he did not know the water rules. In most places you needed a licence to fish. His licence only applied to the river near his home. He was probably poaching, but there was no notice forbidding fishing. He wrapped the fish in his handkerchief and stowed them in his rucksack.

There were rain clouds massing on the horizon. Paddy Joe eyed the stream uneasily. It was the kind that came into sudden spate if rain fell in the hills.

"Never trust water," Tomkin always said, and told him of river beds that ran almost dry one second and in the next a bore of peaty yellow water foamed in torrent from the hills, brought down after a distant thunderstorm.

Paddy Joe removed the lead from Storm's collar, and began to climb. He had seen no one for several hours. He was alone in the world, and the sky was darkening, and the first faint growls of thunder echoed from the hills above him. He had picked a bad time for camping. August was so often stormy, and this was a stormier month than most. He was in one of the little woods and he pretended that he was an army scout in country that had never known man. Pretence was easy because here the trees grew thickly, their slender stems too close, their branches twining, and their cover so dense that underneath was only bare earth, thick with leaf mould. A bird flew from the trees above his head, calling in startled notes that were picked up from beak to beak, until the wood was noisy with anger. It was strange country where the upland hills were bleak but the valleys so thickly wooded that it was possible to pass in moments from wood to bare moor, and seem in a different world.

The first drops of rain pattered through the trees. The day-light had vanished and lightning flashed continuously. It was not safe in the wood. Lightning might strike the trees. Paddy Joe began to run, Storm keeping to heel, over soft, springy ground and out into the open again, beside an overhang of rock.

The ground sloped downwards to the river, and already the water was rising. They were well above it, but they needed shelter from the rain. Wind troubled the branches, lashing the thin trunks; sighing; shrieking; groaning; rushing through the wood; rain lashed from a sky that held no pity in its sullen towering clouds.

Paddy Joe climbed round the overhang. Bushes sheltered a small opening. He shouldered through them, and found a cave. It was no more than a tunnel under a tumble of rock, but it was temporary sanctuary. Here was peace and privacy and somewhere to hide. Here he might perhaps leave Storm and go shopping. On his own he would be unremarkable, another boy where boys were many. With Storm he was conspicuous. He sighed, and leaned against the dog's broad back, and shared the rest of Solomon's food with him.

There was a change of clothing in the rucksack and Paddy Joe removed his wet clothes and dressed more comfortably. The cave was dry and sheltered from the wind and rain.

He slept, using Storm as a living pillow. He was exhausted by the need to think out every move, to plan, not knowing the future, and to stay out of sight. Storm guarded his master, ears cocked, listening alertly, uneasy in such strange surroundings. The dog sighed deeply. His watchful eyes were sad. Life had changed bewilderingly in the last few days. There was no familiar routine; Martha and Grandee had vanished, and all he had was Paddy Joe, and the dog was determined that the boy would not vanish too. Paddy Joe was Storm's anchor, and Storm intended to make quite certain that neither of them was left alone.

Paddy Joe woke and stretched wearily. He ought to make plans. Six more days—or was it five now? It was early afternoon. He must have slept for several hours. Today was Monday. The colonel and Tomkin would be home by Saturday evening. Only five and a half more days.

Paddy Joe was worried. He had laid a trail that any policeman must be able to see. First he had gone with the shepherd who would surely have heard the news bulletin item and told the police of the boy to whom he had given a lift. Or would he not associate Patrick Joseph Rafferty with Pat Jones, and Storm with Riff? Perhaps they had a chance. And what about the saddler? Would he hear, and realise the truth, and inform the police? It was a good job that he had been able to keep Storm out of sight in the shop when the policeman came. And he had to trust Tom Vence and Johnnie Blackett not to give him away.

They needed to push on and to stay out of sight. All the woodcraft that Tomkin had taught him would have to be used. Paddy Joe packed his rucksack. He would have to buy food again soon. He himself could do without but he couldn't starve his dog. Storm wouldn't understand. Perhaps Storm would catch himself a rabbit, if he got really hungry. Perhaps they could catch more fish. The two trout from the morning's fishing would make their supper. Perhaps they would find someone who lived in an isolated place who would let them shelter . . . a farmer who had broken his leg and needed help, or a lonely retired man who had fallen and twisted his ankle . . .

It was no use wishing. Paddy Joe looked about the cave. The only sign of his occupancy was a footmark in the dust, and this he swept away with his handkerchief.

He glanced at his watch. It was just after five, and the rain had made everything sodden. They ploughed through wet bracken. There was a rustle behind them. Storm stiffened. Paddy Joe turned his head to see a fox slipping past, a rabbit in his jaws. He grabbed Storm's collar. The fox glanced towards them and paused, amber eyes gleaming. A bird called in fury and the fox loped on, and they were alone again, except for the wingclap as a pigeon rose in panic, angling away from the fox.

Paddy Joe followed the beast trails. The narrow ways were marked by sheep and fox and badger. He walked carefully. The evening sun split gold across the bracken, etched the shadows of trees at his feet, and teased the leaves, pale flickers of light sliding across the ground as the branches rustled and shifted in the thin cold wind that had succeeded the storm.

The river called to Paddy Joe. He wanted to be beside it and rest, soothed by the lull of the water. He could make a fire and cook the fish that he had caught earlier that day. He loved the sound of running water. It reminded him of home and fishing with Tomkin, and happier days. Storm frolicked gaily, joyous with life.

Paddy Joe found a grassy place, hidden by a thick growth of willow, and dropped to the ground. He had nowhere to go and was in no hurry. One place was as good as another, and there was plenty of cover here. Perhaps he could catch enough fish to make shopping unnecessary. His whole attention was on the water, on the minute ripples and shivers, on a dipper, preening its feathers on a stone, on a swallow balanced on a wire strung between two posts, the sun bright on vivid feathers that were midnight blue and gleaming, seen close under the sparkle of light.

Storm was hunting. There was an unusual scent on the grass, and he chased it, nose down, tail waving, careful never to lose sight of Paddy Joe. He found a mouse, and watched it, but did not attempt to kill it. The tiny beast crouched, paralysed by terror, staring up at the dog that overshadowed everything around him, gasping as the scent of the giant horror poured into nostrils sensitive to every tremor of the wind.

Storm went back to Paddy Joe, and a moment later, the boy stilled the dog, and crouched, arms round his neck, hand over the animal's mouth. He had heard footsteps.

The man who passed was in no hurry. Fishing rod and hamper betrayed his aim, but he had no desire to stay here. He was walking the river bank, noting every curve and twist, every bush that might help him hide from the fish beneath the water, every tree that might snag a line. He was computing the depth and the bottom, looking for pools where fish might lurk, observing the betraying ripple on the water. He had no eyes for anything else and passed so close to Paddy Joe's hiding place that his foot left a mark only two inches from the boy's hand. The fisherman was concentrating on the water, anxious to catch the evening rise.

There was no safety here. When the fisherman had gone, Paddy Joe slipped through the bushes and began to climb. Storm paced beside him. Together they crept through the trees, using every scrap of cover; stopping; listening; watching; anxious not to be seen.

It was slow going, but it was safer than hurrying. Speed would betray them. Speed would spread their shadows in front of them, revealing their hiding places.

Speed would crack branch and rustle twig. Speed would mask the noise of others approaching them.

Paddy Joe wished he had a destination. It was so much easier than running nowhere. Nowhere to go. Not until Brownie and Tomkin came home. If only he knew where they had gone, he might make his way there, but there was a lot of Scotland, and he had not the ghost of an idea.

The evening air was chill. Sunlight died in the woods. Storm chased a moth and came hastily back, recalled sharply to business, but it was hard to be business-like and he was full of life and mischief. The woods had given way to moorland again, and far away there was the thin thread of a main road, where the westering sun reflected off the windscreens of cars, and flashed brightly. Perhaps they might risk asking for a lift. Paddy Joe was not sure. He put on the scout beret. It really depended on how often his own particular little news item had been broadcast, on whether it had been televised together with his picture and Storm's, and on the driver who stopped for him. He could not make up his mind at all.

The road was bordered by a low wall. The grass was dry behind the wall, and Paddy Joe sat, back to the road, disconsolate. Everything was too difficult. If he were discovered now, Storm would be taken from him and he himself taken back, and what sort of punishment was given to boys who ran away? What would Mr Throstle do? Paddy Joe knew that he was unreasonably terrified of the solicitor with his dry as dust manner and his air of never seeing anyone who was less than ninety years old. It was impossible that Mr Throstle had ever been a boy himself. He didn't understand anything.

Storm was watching the grass move. There was a rustle in the undergrowth. There was a noise that only the dog could hear. Paddy Joe was too miserable to notice the dog's alert ears and cocked head and interested expression. Storm's eyes were following the movement. The grass parted and the dog stared. He had never seen anything like the creature that slid towards him before. Limbless, slender, rippling on unseen muscles, diamond back shining in the last rays of sun, bright eyes glittering, the snake turned its head and saw the boy and dog.

The adder was not seeking trouble. It was anxious only to slide away. Storm could not resist the movement. He lifted his paw playfully and laid it heavily on the snake and in that instant the reptile defended itself and struck and Storm yelped in panic as the fangs bit deep.

Paddy Joe leaped to attention. His eyes widened in horror. He had no time to think. His fingers closed on a piece of rock, which he hammered down on the snake's back. The backbone snapped and the creature died, and Storm lay quiet, the skin on his shoulder swelling visibly, his breath distressed.

Paddy Joe had no choice. He did not know if his dog would die, if snake-bite was fatal, if he would be in time. He needed help, and he needed it fast. He jumped to the top of the wall, now desperate to flag down a passing car, and never mind if he were recognised.

The long straight stretch of road was empty for as far as he could see. The dog's panting breath was terrifying. Storm whimpered, and Paddy Joe knelt beside him, listening for the sound of an engine, while he stroked the soft fur. Storm was hidden in a mist that clouded his eyes. His throat ached with misery.

He had run away for nothing. His dog was certain to die.

Chapter Twelve

The swelling was terrifying. Paddy Joe jumped on to the wall. If only someone would come. He needed help desperately. He had never felt so alone in his life. He had no idea what to do. Someone must come. There must be cars along here soon. There had been enough of them before the snake struck. Paddy Joe had been aware of the constant sound of passing engines.

A large grey saloon car approached, the driver changing gear noisily. Paddy Joe waved frantically, but the car was fully loaded, and one of the passengers moved his hand backwards and forwards regretfully. Paddy Joe swallowed, panic very close. Please God, don't let Storm die. Please God, let a car come and take us to a vet. Please God, I'll never run away again.

The lorry that crested the little rise towards him slowed down and Paddy Joe ran forward hopefully, but it did not stop. The driver called through the open window.

"Sorry, son, I'm not allowed to give lifts. I'd get the sack."

The noise of his gear change drowned Paddy Joe's desperate words.

"My dog's been bitten by a snake."

It sounded worse, said out loud. He looked over the wall. Storm was stretched out as if he were dead, but his chest laboured as he breathed. There was another car coming. Paddy Joe looked down the road and saw a dark blue long wheel-base Land-Rover.

It had to stop. It simply had to stop. Paddy Joe ran into the road, frantically waving his beret. The Land-Rover drew up within a few feet of him and the driver jumped out.

"You stupid little idiot. What the blazes are you trying to do? Get killed?"

He was young, and looked like a student. His long hair and side whiskers met a full beard. He wore a tartan shirt tucked into dark green corduroy trousers. He stared at Paddy Joe, his brown eyes angry.

"Go easy on the kid. He's dead scared," the man in the passenger seat protested. He climbed down too, looking searchingly at Paddy Joe. He also was dark, but was clean shaven and his hair, cut neatly at the nape of his neck, had been brushed until it shone. He too wore corduroys, and his green shirt and tie matched them perfectly.

"What's up, Kiddo?"

Paddy Joe gulped. He was shaking, suddenly terrified.

"My dog's been bitten by a snake," he said.

"Grief! Where is he?" The man in the green shirt was already running to the wall. Paddy Joe joined him, and the driver followed, his anger forgotten.

"Poor beast. Get the back of the Land-Rover open, Kiddo, and we'll carry him. The town's only a few minutes away, and there's sure to be a vet."

They were already lifting Storm and Paddy Joe ran and opened the back door of the big Land-Rover. It was fitted out like a caravan with two low bunks and two drop-down bunks above them, that were fastened against the wall. There was a tiny stove and a small sink. The two men lifted Storm on to the bunk, and pushed Paddy Joe in beside him, and ran to the front of the car. Before Paddy Joe had time to gather his wits the Land-Rover was in gear, was turning, and was accelerating back in the direction from which they had come.

Paddy Joe could say nothing. He could not stop shaking, and he could not bear to look at Storm, or listen to him. The dog was almost unconscious, unaware of anything or anyone, beyond the reach of words. Paddy Joe could only stroke the soft fur, and wish he had never run away, never brought Storm to be bitten by a snake and die in pain.

"Cheer up, Kiddo," the man in green said. "Here, drink this." He was pouring coffee from a flask and he handed the beaker to Paddy Joe. "It's hot and sweet and you've had a shock. Your dog'll be OK. Big dogs don't die from snake-bite. It's a good job he's not a terrier. That would be curtains."

The coffee was warming and restoring, and Paddy Joe felt better. A moment later the Land-Rover slowed down.

"There's a policeman with a police dog. He'll know where the vet is." The driver braked and called out.

Paddy Joe thought his heart would stop beating. Suppose the policeman was looking for him? Suppose he prevented them going to the vet? He wanted to scream, but he could only crouch, horrified, and keep his face hidden. He knew that the man in the green shirt was watching him, but he could not, for the life of him, turn and look at the policeman.

"We've a dog here that's been bitten by a snake," the driver said, as the policeman turned towards him.

"That's bad luck." The policeman glanced in through the window at Storm. "The vet's in the main street, about a mile farther on. It's a big house in its own grounds, next to the church. This side of the church. You can't miss it. I'll radio in to the police station and ask them to ring up and tell him you're on your way and he'll have the stuff ready by the time you get there. He has an evening surgery so you're in luck."

The policeman reached out his arm and patted Paddy Joe on the shoulder, and Paddy Joe nearly jumped off the bench he was sitting on.

"Don't worry, son. I know how you feel, but he'll be OK. I promise you. The antidote works like magic. Hurry up and I'll radio the Station to warn him you're coming."

The driver accelerated away from the kerb. Paddy Joe sat dumbly, unable to care any longer whether he was caught or not. His hands smoothed the Alsatian's fur. His brain had stopped working. He noticed, vaguely, that they were passing through a small town, leaving closed shops and deserted street stalls behind them. A moment later he saw the church and the house beside it, and the engraved nameplate on the pillar that had once held iron gates, but that now leaned sideways, as if it had forgotten how to stand erect.

The Land-Rover turned into the drive, and drove over the gravel and braked at the door. A man was waiting for them, a syringe in his hand, and within seconds he was in the van, and bending over the dog.

"Poor old fellow. This'll put him straight in no time, don't you worry," he said. He was a small man, almost bald, his face red with weather, his eyes blue, his manner reassuring. Paddy Joe had not believed the man in the green shirt or the policeman, but he did believe the vet.

"How long before he's better?" he asked, and barely recognised his own voice.

The man straightened up and put a blanket over the dog.

"Keep him warm and quiet. When he's hungry just give him milk for the time being. Bring him for another injection first thing tomorrow morning," the vet said. "He'll be much better then and I'll tell you how to feed him. I'll see you again tomorrow. I'll take particulars then. I've a large surgery tonight and an emergency operation when I've finished."

He hurried inside again, and Paddy Joe stared at the driver and his friend. Life had complicated itself beyond all measure. If only he weren't so tired, and could think what to do.

"Patrick Joseph Rafferty, missing from his home since Thursday morning," the man in green said softly, looking at Paddy Joe.

It was more than he could bear. Tears forced themselves down his cheeks and he turned his head away. The man in green reached out a hand and shook Paddy Joe's shoulder gently.

"OK Kiddo, I just wanted to be sure. Tell us why. That's all. Have you done something you shouldn't have done?"

Paddy Joe shook his head.

It was difficult to speak.

The words came slowly, in the voice that sounded as if it belonged to someone else.

"My grandmother died. They were going to put me in a home and put Storm to sleep. I only wanted to hide till the colonel came home."

"Food," the man in green said suddenly. "Come on, Steve. Drive to a quiet lay-by and let's eat. I bet the kid's starving. We can talk then."

Steve drove out of the gate and in a few minutes they were outside the town, and back on the road where Paddy Joe had flagged them down. There was a big lay-by, and Steve parked the vehicle.

"I'm Chris," said the man in green, "and this is Steve, and you're Patrick and your dog's called Storm."

"My friends always call me Paddy Joe," Paddy Joe said.

"Good enough. Steve's a dab hand with the frying pan. You tell me about yourself while he cooks, and you can drink some more coffee, and have it sweet this time, too. You look all in, Kiddo."

The coffee tasted wonderful. Paddy Joe had not realised how much he had missed hot drinks, and by now the evening was cold. Darkness had come unawares. The moon played tag with the clouds, and a few faraway stars gleamed in the gaps in the racing masses that were building once more to bring rain. The wind sighed on the moor, and whined in the wires. The town lay behind them, a glow on the horizon, and they were marooned, isolated, in the lighted Land-Rover cabin, while Storm lay without moving, and panted horribly, so that Paddy Joe wished he could stop the noise and soothe the dog.

"He doesn't know anything, and he's not in pain now. He's asleep."

Chris was essentially kind. He had two small brothers, and he knew how Paddy Joe felt. Steve was busy frying eggs and bacon and tomatoes and mushrooms on a tiny two-ringed stove powered by a Calor gas cylinder tucked neatly under one of the bunks.

"Tell us," Chris said, and Paddy Joe found it a relief to talk, to talk of home and the colonel, and of Tomkin and Mr Throstle. Of Willie Brakewell and Tom Vence and Johnnie Blackett and the saddler. Such a lot had happened in the last few days. Chris listened, asking a question here and there, and Steve found plates and piled them with food and tucked himself into a corner and listened too.

"It's Storm I'm worried about," Paddy Joe said. He looked at the dog.

"You can stay with us," Chris said. "OK, Steve?"

Steve nodded, his mouth too full to speak. He was very quiet, and rarely spoke. Chris did most of the talking for both of them and also seemed to make most of the decisions.

"We're students," Chris said. "Steve is going to be an engineer and I'm doing law. We've been farming, to get some money for next term and help our grants stretch, and now we're planning a few days camping before we get back to work. We've a lot of swotting to do before term begins in October, as this is our final year. Degree exams at the end of it. Wow! It's an awful thought," he added.

"Appalling," Steve said soberly, and grinned at Paddy Joe.

"No one expects us back, and Steve's Dad lent us the Land-Rover," Chris said. "We intended to go off into the blue, and we can do just that. We can sleep here tonight, and in the morning take Storm for his injection. By then he ought to be well enough for us to go off. There are four bunks, so there's no problem there. We'll take you back to the colonel on Saturday night. How about that?"

It sounded too good to be true. It solved everything, for the time being at least. There would be new problems to face when he got back. The colonel might not want Storm. It might still have been for nothing. But he had a chance now. If only Storm recovered from the snake venom. Paddy Joe nodded, unable to say any of the words that were forming in his head, wishing he could say thank you another way, because the everyday phrase was not enough. Chris guessed his thoughts and pressed his shoulder again, and the moment passed.

That night Paddy Joe lay on the top bunk above Storm and listened to the dog's breathing. Steve snored and Chris slept restlessly, tossing and turning. Cars passed, close to the lay-by, and the threatened rain came in gusts and flurries, drumming on the metal roof, a ceaseless background of sound that kept Paddy Joe awake long into the night. When he slept, he dreamed that Storm had become very ill and was whining horribly. He started up as Steve, looking like a tousled heron, switched on the light and stared at the dog.

Storm's desperate whimper had wakened them all.

Chapter Thirteen

Storm whined again.

He felt horrible. His throat was dry and he was very thirsty. His shoulder was on fire and his legs ached and he wanted to go outside. When he tried to stand he discovered he was in a strange and peculiar place; that he could smell, but could not see, Paddy Joe; that his legs wouldn't work properly; and that his bark had vanished and the only noise he could make was a thin desperate whimper.

"He's worse," Paddy Joe said. He had jumped down to stand beside his dog. Storm lifted his head and tried to lick Paddy Joe's hand. His tail made a small movement.

"He's better," Chris said. "The swelling's much less and I expect he's thirsty and wants to go outside."

He clambered down from his bunk, and Steve joined him. They lifted the dog to the ground. He did want to go out, and a few minutes later they lifted him inside again, and Chris filled a bowl with milk and held it for the Alsatian. Storm drank as if he had never been able to drink before. Paddy Joe could not believe his eyes. The dog finished his drink, and, exhausted, flopped down on the bunk. His breathing was easier, but he could not yet move properly. He was content, knowing that Paddy Joe was near. Steve switched off the light. Paddy Joe climbed down from his own bunk and tucked in to the lower one, pulling the blanket over both of them. There was not much room. He did not care. Storm's warm body was beside him, and the dog's tongue was wet and reassuring on his cheek. He fell so deeply asleep that they were on their way to the vet before he opened his eyes, bewildered to find his bed moving, and his horizon bordered by trees that flashed past the window.

Paddy Joe climbed stiffly down from the bunk. Storm sat up groggily and stared out of the window.

"He's miles better," Steve said.

"Patient doing fine," said Chris. He grinned at Paddy Joe.

"I thought you might like to change," he added. "Your clothes look rather a mess and for the next few days you're my young brother. It's lucky we're both dark. Try those for size." He pointed to a heap of clothing on the other bunk. Paddy Joe found a pair of corduroys that were somewhat large, but cleaner than his own jeans, and a bright tartan shirt that fitted loosely but did not look bad tucked into the trouser tops. Everything he had been wearing looked in need of a good wash.

The sun was shining and the day already warm as the Land-Rover turned into the vet's drive. This time, Storm was able to walk, although he obviously felt wobbly, and once or twice he staggered. Paddy Joe followed Chris and Steve into the waiting-room, as they felt he was unlikely to be noticed as part of a group of three, and Storm was not willing to follow either of them. He wanted to be sure that Paddy Joe was in sight. The dog felt ill and was in strange company, and he was determined to keep contact with the one familiar part of his life.

The people in the waiting-room admired the big Alsatian, and were startled to hear he was suffering from snake-bite.

"Has he had any food?" the vet asked, as they came into the surgery.

"A lot of water, and a little milk," Chris said.

"If he's hungry, give him fish," the vet said. "I wouldn't give him meat for a day or two yet. He'll probably only want milk for the time being. It's lucky the bite wasn't on his throat. You would've had trouble then."

Storm sat patiently waiting for his injection.

"Sorry, feller," the vet said. "Most dogs hate this," he added. "One dog bit me last week. I ought to have muzzled him, but his owner said he was quiet." He laughed. "I should've known. He had that look about him. You can usually tell."

"Sto——he never bit anyone," Paddy Joe said, remembering just in time not to say "Storm". It had nearly slipped out. Storm, to show he had no ill feelings about being stabbed with a needle, licked the vet's hand.

"That's the kind of dog I appreciate," the vet said, and patted the Alsatian. "He's a splendid creature."

"He's very obedient," Paddy Joe said.

"He could give lessons to some of the dogs I know," the vet said and added, "That will be one pound and twenty-five pence."

It was nearly all the money that Paddy Joe had left. It was a good job that Johnnie Blackett had lent him some. He could at least pay for his own dog's treatment, and not be indebted to Chris and Steve.

The vet paid the money into the till. His next words almost floored Paddy Joe.

"Name and address, please," he said.

Paddy Joe stared up at Chris, who quietly interpreted the agonised glance.

"Chris Turner, Honeydale Cottage, Store Lane, Leeds," he said.

The vet wrote it down without question.

"You're some way from home," he commented.

"We're camping," Chris said. "One last fling before getting down to swot for finals next summer."

"Make the most of it," the vet said, grinning. He looked at Paddy Joe, "You'll not be doing your finals for some time, son. D'you know what you're going to be?"

Paddy Joe had never even thought what he was going to be. He looked at the vet and he looked at Storm, who was already so much better, and who was now sitting with perked up ears, his eyes brighter, his legs obviously beginning to belong to him again. It had been the vet's knowledge that had made this possible, and Paddy Joe quite suddenly knew, without any doubt, what he intended to be when he grew up.

"I'm going to be a vet," he said determinedly.

The vet looked at him, considering.

"Are you, now?" he said. "I hope you keep to that, but make no mistake, son, it's one of the hardest careers there is. As difficult as being a doctor. Perhaps more so, because a doctor only has to know about people and their illnesses, and people can tell him where the pain is. In addition, the vet has to know about every kind of animal. Cows don't have the same troubles as cats, and dogs are different again. Swine fever is nothing like fowl pest, and all animals have different kinds of insides. A cow is nothing like a pig, nor a rabbit like a bird. You can give a dog a tranquilliser without much fear, but give one to a cat and you never know what'll happen; I've known one go gently to sleep and wake up like a baby afterwards, and another almost paralysed by the same dose, and another that raced round and round the room and climbed the curtains. You never know what'll happen next, either, and you have to work all day and a great many nights too."

"I still want to be a vet," Paddy Joe said. It was something to work for, to dream about, a goal to aim at, a reason for going on and on, learning at school and out of school. He knew that many of the things that Tomkin had taught him about dogs and horses would be very useful when he was a vet. From now on, animals would form a major part of his life. He wasn't sure how, but somehow.

"Good for you," the vet said. "Come back and see me when you qualify, and I'll give you a job."

He laughed as he spoke, but Paddy Joe intended to do just that. One day, he would be a real vet himself and make other people's animals better. It was a resolve that hardened as he thought. It was a beginning of something that would be a major part of his life, and it had happened just after the most miserable days of his life. One thing led to another, but it was queer that Storm being bitten by a snake should show him the path that his future would take.

"If he doesn't improve, bring him back. But you shouldn't have any more trouble," the vet said, and Storm led the way out, his tail once more high and proudly waving. He stopped and looked back at the vet, and barked once.

"He's saying thank you," Paddy Joe said. A small wave of elation thrilled him, and he took Storm's collar and led the dog back to the Land-Rover.

"Now we can all celebrate," Chris said, as they drove on to the road again. "We'll take you out for the meal of your life, in one of those restaurants where the lights are so low you can't see what you're eating, let alone what faces look like. No one will notice you in the gloom. Storm can stay on his bunk, and you can relax. I bet you've been as tight as wet string for the last few days, haven't you?"

Paddy Joe nodded.

It was not easy to believe he was safe even now. A moment later he knew that he was not. He had been living in a dream. This was real life. Things never did go right. They had come to the traffic lights, and as the light changed to green a small van drew up beside them and a voice shouted.

"Draw in on the other side of the lights. I'd like a word with you."

It was the policeman who had spoken to them the day before. Chris looked at Steve. Paddy Joe's mouth was dry. His hands were wet with sweat. He tried to swallow and felt extremely sick as Chris drew in to the kerb and parked neatly. The policeman parked in front of them, and, as he jumped out, his dog barked. Storm lifted his head, and cocked it on one side, his ears pricked, listening. Paddy Joe gave him a quick signal. The policeman walked over to the driver's window and looked inside. Paddy Joe's heart began to thump. He wanted to run. He had never thought that the sight of a blue uniform could be so frightening. His knees were shaking.

"How did you get on, yesterday? Is your dog all right?" The man's voice was friendly and unsuspicious. Chris was watching Paddy Joe, who went so white with relief, that the student thought the boy was going to faint. The policeman intercepted the glance and a faint frown appeared on his face. Chris, seeing it, jumped hurriedly to the rescue.

"I think we just got there in time," Chris said, "We've all had a pretty sticky night. The dog belongs to my kid brother and I think he's suffering from shock as much as the Alsatian."

"It's a beautiful dog," the policeman said. "I'm glad he's recovering. What's his name?" "Storm," said Chris, without thinking. "Riff," said Paddy Joe hastily.

The policeman looked at him sharply and his eyebrows went up. "Don't you know your own dog's name?" he asked.

"It's just one of those things," Chris said. "My mother named the dog, and Buster, here, never liked the name. He's an obstinate sort of little cuss. The dog's registered now as Storm—Heathercroft Storm of Lashlight, but the kid always calls him Riff."

"I heard there was a boy begging lifts on this road yesterday," the policeman said. "And there's a boy missing from his home, Patrick Joseph Rafferty, with an Alsatian dog called Storm."

The end of the world had come. It had all been for nothing. He was caught, fair and square, good and proper, and the adventure had ended. He and Storm would be taken away. He would have to face Mr Throstle. He would have to go to the Boys' Home in the city. And that would be the end of Storm. Hope was dead. The sunny morning was overcast and a thin trickle of rain dampened the policeman's helmet, and, sliding down the windscreen, darkened the world. Paddy Joe did not know if it was only the light that had changed or if it was his own terror that was clouding the landscape. He was drowning in misery.

A moment later he realised that Chris was explaining to the policeman.

"Yes, the kid was trying to hitch a lift yesterday. We put him down so that the dog could get some exercise while Steve and I went shopping. It never occurred to us that anything would go wrong, so we didn't hurry. I went and had my hair cut, so that we were much longer than we expected. The kid got scared when the dog was bitten and was afraid that we wouldn't come in time. He's a panicky little beggar at the best of times. I got worked up, too, as I know Mum would blame it on me if anything happened to either of them. Trouble is, young Sid's always in scrapes, and I get blamed for it."

Paddy Joe took a deep breath. He was not at all sure that he liked being christened Sid, or being called a panicky little beggar, but it sounded good, and the policeman had relaxed and was grinning.

"I've got a kid brother, too," he said. "They're a pest, aren't they?" He leaned into the Land-Rover and tugged gently at Paddy Joe's ear.

"I bet you had a real shock didn't you? I know how I feel when my dog's ill. Never mind. Alsatians are pretty tough, and it's all over now. On your way home are you?"

"We're camping for a few days first," Chris said.

"Enjoy yourselves. And watch out for snakes. I should make that big fellow of yours rest for a bit," he said. "Don't let him chase rabbits."

He walked back to his van, but for a moment, none of the three dared breathe. They watched as the policeman executed a U-turn and they answered his wave.

"Phew!" said Chris. "I thought we'd had it then," he laughed. "How are you doing, young Sid?"

"I should have told you," Paddy Joe said. "I'm Pat Jones, and this is Riff."

"Well, you're Sid Turner, now," said Chris. "We'll have to stick to that. The policeman's probably made a note of our number and if he does get suspicious he may check. It depends how closely he checks. The vet has our address, too. I have got a young brother called Sid, but Mum's got a poodle called Cindy. And it was a bit batty to make up a kennel name, especially to a man with a dog of his own, as he may check the kennel club registration. We'll just have to hope for the best and keep off the main roads, and hope we can slip out of sight for a day or two." It was not going to be so easy after all. In spite of that, he determined to make the best of the next few days. At least he was no longer alone.

Chris was good company and though Steve was quiet, he laughed often and easily when Chris told some outrageous story. He was telling one now, as they drove along, a quite silly tale about a little dragon called Rary. The dragon grew and grew and grew and grew and every time he sneezed, he sneezed fire, and burned a town, until there were so few towns left everyone got desperate. The dragon was desperate too as he never meant to hurt anyone. Finally the few remaining people took the dragon up to the very top of Everest, intending to throw him over a precipice. The dragon wanted to know, very sadly, if they were trying to get rid of him and when they said yes, he looked down. Down and down and down and down, to the plains far below, and he said in a very mournful voice,

"It's a long long way to Tipperary; it's a long long way to go!"

There was a small startled silence before everyone laughed, and Steve, grinning wickedly, said,

"Just for that you can buy us lunch. It's the worst pun I've ever heard."

Chris relaxed. He had made Paddy Joe laugh and that was all he had intended. He felt desperately sorry for him. Poor little devil, he'd had a raw deal. Chris had two parents and two brothers and two sisters, and his big noisy family, though often annoying, was great fun most of the time, and was enormous comfort when things went wrong. It must be awful to have nobody. He was tempted to take both boy and dog back to his mother, but his sisters could never keep a secret, and Paddy Joe was safer with him and Steve. They could spend the rest of the time high on the moors, on the mountains where no one ever came. That was the best of the Land-Rover, as they could get off the road and find complete privacy and could stock up with enough food to tide them over for the next four days as well.

Those four days became a memorable part of Paddy Joe's life. When they were certain that Storm was recovering and not in need of more veterinary attention, they left the lowlands, and drove to the hills, climbing high along rutted roads that had rarely seen a car. Here, where the world was empty of houses, and the curlew sang his lonely song, and only sheep turned to watch them as they drove by, they stopped beside a little waterfall. The mountains were all about them, and far away, through a narrow pass, was the incredible blue of the distant sea.

Heather, in purple flower, surrounded them. The rocky outcrops were orange with lichen, and only the wind and water made any noise. Paddy Joe was able to relax, to be a boy again, to climb to the peak above them and look at the world spread out as far as he could see, looking down on road and town and moor, and to the sea that almost encircled them. He grew to know Chris and Steve better. Steve liked to think, and dream, and to read, and spoke rarely, although he was always ready to laugh at Chris. Steve had a deep brooding temper, and was sometimes angry, but nothing seemed to ruffle Chris, who loved talking, and telling outrageous jokes that nearly always ended with a pun, and loved singing. He had a good tenor voice, and in the evening, they lay on the grass outside the Land-Rover, while Storm kept close to Paddy Joe, and Steve played his flute, and Chris sang.

It was wonderful to lie and listen, with nothing but the sky above them, and a moonglow over the hills, and the remote stars looking down. Both men loved the old folk-songs, and the Irish tunes and the Scottish tunes that Grandee had also loved. Paddy Joe, lying with a piece of heather in his hands, and Storm's head on his knee, listened to "Down by the Sally Gardens" and "I'm off to Philadelphia" and some of the Scottish Songs of the Isles, and felt at peace and at home for the first time since his grandmother had died. He wished he had an elder brother, and envied Chris's youngest brother, the real Sid, who was also twelve and, who, judging by the stories Chris told about him, must be quite one of the naughtiest boys who had ever lived.

The days passed unbelievably fast. They ate breakfast at nine, and then walked, or swam in a pool below the waterfall, the water so cold that it took their breath away. Steve, who enjoyed cooking, prepared lunch for them all. They had stocked themselves with plenty of tinned food before leaving the town, and had bought tinned milk so that they need not show themselves at any farm.

The afternoons were spent reading. Paddy Joe nearly finished the *Lord of the Rings*, and Chris took out a book on law, while Steve studied a very dull looking book on engineering machinery. They lay on the grass in the sun, leaning against small rocks that provided convenient backrests, while Storm slept, or prowled lazily in search of exciting smells. Paddy Joe noticed that the dog was much more careful when he was hunting, and that he shied away anxiously from any thick twig or branch that curled, snake-like. He didn't intend to be bitten again. Once Steve had found a length of thin rope lying on the ground, and carried it, swinging from his hand, to the Land-Rover, thinking it might come in handy for something. Storm was asleep by the step, and woke to see the rope dangling above his head. He jumped up and backed away, growling savagely, so that Paddy Joe came running, never having heard his dog behave like that before. It was a moment before any of them realised what was wrong, and then Paddy Joe took the rope and showed it to the Alsatian, who sat down, his sheepish expression back on his face, as much to say I'm sorry I was such a fool.

"It will be a long day before he trusts anything snaky again," Chris said. "Just as well. It shows he's learned and that's one danger you won't have to worry about."

On the evening of the second day, the Thursday of that week, Chris, going into the Land-Rover, made a sudden face.

"I don't want to complain," he said. "But there's something in here that stinks. I suppose Storm wouldn't catch anything and hide it?"

"Of course not," Paddy Joe said indignantly. He climbed in beside Chris. There was a quite horrible and most extraordinary smell.

Steve added his sniffs to theirs, and Chris, more practically, began to sniff at everything inside the Land-Rover. Storm, seeing them, joined in too, and suddenly pointed his nose at Paddy Joe's rucksack and barked.

"Paddy Joe, what on earth are you hiding in there?" Steve demanded. "It smells fair awful!"

"Take it outside," Chris said. "For goodness sake, what have you got hidden in there?"

Paddy Joe could not imagine. He tossed everything out on to the grass. A dirty shirt. His socks and spare jersey, and . . .

"Oh help," he said in dismay, and Steve and Chris, looking over his shoulder, burst out laughing.

"Paddy Joe's emergency rations," Steve said. "Oh lord. What a stink."

Storm barked.

"I'm not jolly well surprised," said Steve. "It's not everyone that carries dead trout around in a rucksack for days on end."

The trout were very dead indeed, and everything smelled of bad fish. Paddy Joe had completely forgotten about them. He looked at them in dismay. Chris fetched the spade and took the rotten fish and dug a hole and buried them, and Paddy Joe took his rucksack and clothes over to the waterfall and tried to wash the smell away, but it lingered horribly.

"Spread them in the air," Chris said. "It'll go. You are a little chump, Paddy Joe."

Paddy Joe had to agree, but next day he managed to earn their approval, as, determined to make up for his silliness, he took his reel and line to the little stream below the waterfall, and began to fish in earnest. There was a deep pool beyond the bank, inside a pot hole, and he caught eight trout, and brought them proudly to Steve to cook for lunch. It made a change from tinned food, and, grilled, with fried potatoes, and tomatoes, it was a meal fit for a king, and more than made up for the awful smell that was now fading.

If only there had not been the faint niggling worry at the back of Paddy Joe's mind he would have been completely happy. Chris and Steve were fun, and he had never spent much time with people near his own age. Grandee and the colonel and Tomkin were all very old, compared with Paddy Joe, and he had never had friends to stay as Martha and Grandee found one boy a handful. Two would have been more than they could manage. Though he had school friends, he lived too far away to go to visit them for tea, as there was only the school bus that came anywhere near his home, and Grandee would not ask the colonel to let Tomkin drive Paddy Joe to his friends, and she would not let him have a bicycle either. She was too worried about the traffic on the roads.

It was fun to lie in the sunshine and hear Chris talk about his family; about his father, who was a chemical engineer in a big factory, and his mother, who had trained as a nurse, and now that her family were almost grown, had gone back to work in a busy hospital for three days a week.

He told Paddy Joe about his two sisters, both married, one with a small daughter of almost three, who loved animals more than anything else in the world, so that Chris took her to the Zoo whenever he was home, every Saturday. She knew the names of every animal there, and had given most of them names of her own as well. She called the warthog Diamond, which amused Steve immensely, so that he laughed out loud, something he rarely did. She had a new kitten called Pinkie, although he was black, because pink was her favourite colour, and she had a toy Panda called Micky Tom Dolittle, because she liked looking at the pictures in Sid's Dr Dolittle books. Her books were all about animals.

Steve, like Paddy Joe, was an only child, and listened with as much fascination as Paddy Joe to the tales of a big, noisy family. Later, on the last night of all, when Chris finished talking, they lay and watched a near full moon paint the hills with light and outline the edges of distant clouds with brilliance, and shine on the river, silvering it to a metallic sheen. The surge and swirl and suck of water formed a background to the slow notes of Steve's flute. Storm moved close to Paddy Joe and sighed deeply and dropped his head on the boy's thigh. He had almost recovered from the snake-bite, but he was easily tired, and obviously not yet completely fit. Paddy Joe stroked the soft ears, and knew that the Alsatian too was listening to the music.

Chris began to sing. The words drifted into the air, and echoed from the hills. There was magic abroad in the night. The flute was a lulling, soothing, drifting swirl of music; it was Pan Pipes, calling to the creatures of the wild; it was the song of Orpheus, thrilling every beast that heard it. Paddy Joe was suddenly aware that the sheep were listening too, as moonlight glinted on eyes that had not been there a moment before, and shone on woolly backs.

There was moonlight all around, and starlight high above, and music that danced, and lagged and rose and fell on the air. Paddy Joe, lying on his groundsheet on the grass, drifted into sleep. In after years, when the moon was full and the stars were high, he felt Storm's weight against him, and heard, in memory, the soft call of Steve's flute and the deep full tones of Chris's voice, and remembered how happy he had been, out there in the night, remote from home, although an uncertain future was only a pulse beat away.

Chapter Fourteen

Storm woke Paddy Joe. They had fallen asleep lying on the grass. The moon had vanished in a swathe of dense cloud, the wind was rising, and a splatter of rain flurried from the sky. Paddy Joe roused Chris and Steve and they all climbed into bed without bothering to undress. Steve shut the door as Storm jumped inside, and Paddy Joe lay awake for a while, listening to the wind howling eerily round the Land-Rover.

He woke to a grey day, with rain teeming from a sodden sky. They cooked breakfast and tidied up. Chris and Paddy Joe washed up while Steve looked through his maps and plotted their route. Paddy Joe could guide them once they reached his school, but until then it was unfamiliar country to all of them.

Saturday. Today the colonel and Tomkin would come home. Today Storm's fate would finally be decided. Today time had run right out and the choice no longer lay with Paddy Joe. He sat miserably on his bunk, as the Land-Rover descended from the clouds that now surrounded them, so that driving was a nightmare, and mist swirled across the road and the windscreen wipers played an incessant maddening tune. Today you'll find out. Today you'll find out. Today you'll find out. Paddy Joe began to feel sick.

He did not want to leave the hills and reach the main road, but they were there all too soon, driving in Saturday traffic, car after car, nose to bumper, stop and start and stop and start again, unable to travel far. Once they were held up by a herd of cows; once there was a mile long traffic jam due to road repairs; once a long slow crawl caused by traffic lights that had ceased to function and had been replaced by a policeman.

They would never get home at all at this rate and Paddy Joe did not know whether to be glad or sorry when Steve finally said he needed a rest, and pulled into a lay-by. Chris made coffee and they ate meat pies that he had bought in a baker's in one of the villages on the way. Paddy Joe was certain that every mouthful would choke him, but he did not want the two friends to know how he felt, so he chewed and swallowed, but he might as well have been eating cardboard. Storm lay on the grass fighting a big marrow bone. It must be nice to be a dog, Paddy Joe thought. Storm had no idea of the worries that bothered his master. He only knew that he was feeling well for the first time since the snake had bitten him and that he had a big bone and was enjoying every minute of it. He began to worry the bone and growl at it playfully and Paddy Joe thought that he would not be able to bear one more moment of the day. He dared not wonder what the colonel would say. He could think of nothing but Mr Throstle who had achieved giant size, with grotesquely enormous shiny black boots and a longer-than-real thin nose that twitched and immensely angry hot dark eyes that seared Paddy Joe with their fury.

By teatime it was obvious that they would not reach the colonel's home that day, as the Land-Rover ran over a large jagged nail and developed a puncture that Chris could not repair. They had to stop at a garage. The garage was busy and they could not have the tyre back until the middle of the next morning. There was nothing for it but to find a quiet lane nearby, and drive off the road, and make camp for the night. By now Paddy Joe's unease had begun to affect Chris and Steve. Paddy Joe wanted to telephone. He knew the colonel's number and there was a kiosk at the end of the lane, but although he waited for some minutes, and dialled three times, there was no reply. He could hear the telephone ringing in an empty house. No one answered. It was high time that they were home. A new worry came to take the place of the old. Suppose something had happened to the colonel?

By morning, Paddy Joe was so worried that he was irritable, and was so afraid of snapping at Chris and Steve that he said very little at all. He ate half a piece of toast at breakfast, and could not finish his egg. Neither Chris nor Steve knew quite what to do about him. They guessed how he was feeling, but that was no comfort. Neither of them knew the colonel, or how he would react to a boy who had run away. He might think that it was better for Storm to be put to sleep and Paddy Joe to go and live with other boys of his own age. He might not want the dog at all. Both Chris and Steve by now were fond of Storm, and Steve wondered if his own parents might take the dog, but it was unlikely. His mother would never let him have a small dog, let alone a big one, and Chris's parents had a dog already and would certainly not take a second.

They collected the tyre and set off once more on the road that led to Paddy Joe's home. It was odd to retrace his steps, to drive through the town where Solomon Hasty had his shop, and out again on to the moorland road that he had plodded along so slowly after Johnnie Blackett had driven away. They passed the end of the road that led to Johnnie Blackett's farm; and saw the cliff that Paddy Joe had climbed with Vence, and, at the bottom of the long slope that led into the valley, Paddy Joe looked up and saw the aqueduct and the tunnel entrance, and remembered the sour smell and the choking dark and the black slimy water that flowed sluggishly along the trough.

They climbed out of the valley again, past the shop where Mrs Turner had eyed Paddy Joe so suspiciously. From the back of the Land-Rover Paddy Joe could see over the wall, and see the canal, and see also a narrow boat that chugged along it. He wondered where Tom Vence and Spot were. There was no sign of them on the canal bank.

There was so much holiday traffic that driving was frustratingly slow. Paddy Joe began to count the number of cars towing caravans, and the number towing boats. There were people with speedboats, covered with tarpaulin, huge outboard engines tipped carefully upwards; there were cars with canoes on top of them; cars carrying fibre-glass dinghies on the roofrack; two cars towing quite sizeable small yachts, the masts projecting backwards and marked with white hand-kerchiefs to warn the vehicles behind.

At one intersection a caravan towbar had broken and van and car blocked the road, so that it was necessary to wait for nearly forty minutes before the policeman had sorted out the muddle it had caused. Steve stopped for lunch. Driving was exhausting under such conditions. Paddy Joe drank his coffee and played with the food. If only they could get home. He saw a telephone kiosk on the other side of the road, and once more tried to telephone. Once more he heard the ringing bell. Nobody answered. Neither Chris nor Steve needed to ask if there had been any reply as he lagged miserably across the road, and sat on the wall bordering the lay-by, chewing a grass stalk and wishing that the world would end and he need not worry any more. Storm came and butted his knee and Paddy Joe had to turn his back on the Land-Rover in case he started to cry. Life had become unbearable.

It was nearly four o'clock when they reached Paddy Joe's school and were on familiar ground. The school was closed, the playground empty, the buildings deserted. It added to the feeling of unreality. Paddy Joe directed them through the little town, and out on to heathland. They were not very far from the river where he and Tomkin fished. He had thought it like the Brandywine, a friendly happy place. Now everywhere was suddenly unreal; he no longer belonged. There was no one left that he knew. Something must have happened to the colonel while he was away. In any event, there would be no more fishing expeditions. No more waiting in the early dawn for Tomkin to bring the hunters for exercise. No more riding beside the colonel over the heath, listening to the stories of his army life. The weather echoed Paddy Joe's dismal mood. There was a fine rain falling, that silvered the leaves and made snail trails on the tree trunks, and trickled down the windscreen. The sky was dirty grey, an even colour that masked the blue. Sunshine had gone from the world, along with happiness.

"Cheer up, Kiddo," Chris said but Paddy Joe could not cheer up. He felt even more desolate than before. The sight of familiar places emphasised the fact that he would have to go away. There he had waited for the school bus, Storm beside him, and there he had come home at night, to be greeted by his dog, ardent with delight because Paddy Joe had come back after a long day spent apart. He would no longer see his dog waiting for him, whatever happened now. The lump in his throat had swollen to choke him. He could not have spoken if he had wanted to. He pointed to the end of the lane where the colonel lived, and Steve drove towards the old stone cottage.

Paddy Joe had always loved the colonel's cottage. It was small, black and white, old and thatched. It had been built in Shakespeare's time. The rooms were low and the ceilings timbered with black oak beams that

Tomkin oiled until they gleamed. The big fireplaces were built for logs, and the colonel burned wood on them. The smell of woodsmoke, the gleam of antique furniture, the sound of the grandfather clock, all were vivid in Paddy Joe's mind. He looked out of the window eagerly, as they reached the gate.

He sat numbly, unable to believe his eyes.

The windows were closed, the shutters downstairs were in place, and there was no sign of anybody at all. The colonel had not come home.

Paddy Joe stared, disbelief in his eyes.

Steve looked at Chris. They had come a long way and all for nothing. Neither of them knew what to do next.

"I'm sorry, Paddy Joe," Chris said. "I know now just how a hunted fox feels when he comes home and finds his earth has been stopped."

Chapter Fifteen

Steve reversed the Land-Rover and drove back on to the main road.

"We'd better go and see if there is anyone in your old home," he said. "You can't keep on running, Paddy Joe. We don't want to turn you over to the authorities, but what else can we do?"

"Nothing," Paddy Joe said. He felt as if the world had ended already. It was like a dream in which you fell and landed with a horrible thump and a jump, and woke feeling sick and frightened. Only this time he was awake. This time he was living a nightmare and even if he pinched himself he wouldn't wake up. This time he had to face facts, no matter how unpleasant. If he had not run away everything would be settled by now. Running away had solved nothing. It had altered nothing. Everything was exactly the same as it had been twelve days ago, except that it was complicated by his own actions. It was worse than before, and he had thought then that nothing could be worse. He had been wrong.

Steve drove into the rutted lane that led to Paddy Joe's old home. The trees sheltered them from the rain and parts of the road were dry. Storm, scenting familiar smells, jumped up excitedly and looked out of the window, his tail wagging in frenzy. Paddy Joe clenched his fists and bit his lips. Every minute was torment. He could not look out and see his home and the apple tree, and know the house was up for sale, and that he would never live there again.

Storm rushed from one window to the other. He was coming home. He could smell the garden and the house, and he could smell the bushes by the gate. He could smell something else too, above the smell of petrol from the Land-Rover. He began to bark.

"Quiet," said Paddy Joe.

Storm had no intention of being obedient. He had something to say and no one was listening. He pawed Paddy Joe's leg frantically. They were almost at the gate.

"Is this it?" Steve asked.

Paddy Joe nodded.

Steve drew up and opened the Land-Rover door and was almost knocked flat as the Alsatian leaped over the back of the driver's seat and bounded out, barking ecstatically.

"He certainly knows he's home," Chris said.

From just inside the hedge there came a rustle. Storm jumped over the closed garden gate. His frenzied barks continued, and a voice suddenly said,

"Storm! Storm! Where in the world've you sprung from?"

Paddy Joe tumbled out of the Land-Rover and ran at the gate. It resisted him maddeningly and he pushed hard, and raced through.

"Tomkin! Tomkin!" he shouted.

Tomkin turned away from the dog and saw Paddy Joe. He ran towards him and grabbed him by the shoulders and shook him backwards and forwards gently.

"Paddy Joe! You little idiot, where the dickens've you been? We've had the police out for you, we've ridden the moors till dark every night, we've dragged the river. We've hunted high and low. Even Mr Throstle's been worried sick."

"He wants to put Storm to sleep," Paddy Joe said.

168

He could think of nothing else. It was too horrible to contemplate.

"Well, he can't do it," said Tomkin, and Paddy Joe stared up to him, unable to believe what he had heard. Quite suddenly the world about him began to roar in his ears, and Tomkin grew unaccountably large and then small and Paddy Joe heard his own voice, incredibly distant, as if it belonged to someone else.

"Storm," he whispered, "Storm."

Tomkin's arms were round his shoulders. Chris and Steve had come into the garden, and Chris came forward and lifted Paddy Joe as if he were a baby.

"He didn't want to come home till you were home," Chris said. "He telephoned twice and no one answered, and when we drove up to the colonel's house, he saw that nobody was there."

"Bring him indoors," Tomkin said. He whistled Storm to his side. Paddy Joe's legs refused to work at all. He was shaking, and he wanted to shout and laugh and cry all together. He was glad of Chris's strong grip, and he wondered what on earth had happened to him. He ought to have been rushing round with joy. Instead he could barely move and couldn't speak either.

He was put on the settee in the familiar sitting-room. A fire glowed in the grate, and nothing had changed, except that Grandee was gone, and instead of her rocking-chair was the wing chair from the colonel's home. A moment later the colonel himself came into the room, and knelt beside the settee and took both Paddy Joe's hands firmly in his own. Tomkin took Chris and Steve into the kitchen to find out what had happened to Paddy Joe and to help him make tea.

"If only you'd waited till morning before you ran off," the colonel said. "I saw the notice of your grand-mother's death in the paper, and we came home at once. We arrived about three hours after you'd gone."

"I didn't want to go to the Home," Paddy Joe said. "And I didn't want Storm to be put to sleep."

He was so bewildered now that nothing seemed right yet.

"He won't be," the colonel said, knowing it was the most important part of Paddy Joe's statement. "And you're going to live with me. My lease on the cottage has ended and the landlord wants to sell it. I was going to have to move soon anyway, and so I'm buying your grandmother's house."

Paddy Joe still could not believe any of it. He was safe, and going to live in his old home, and Storm was safe too. The colonel walked over to the fire and poked it, and Paddy Joe watched him, not wanting to lose sight of him, of his tall, lean figure, in brown boots and breeches and hacking jacket, of the face that always reminded Paddy Joe of a saint in a church window, with its long aquiline nose and brooding bushy eyebrows and deep-set dark eyes. The colonel's white hair and moustache contrasted with the brown of his skin. Storm walked over to the hearthrug and spread himself in his usual place against the wall, out of the way of feet that might trip over him. He sighed deeply and curled to sleep, finding life understandable again.

"Throstle's a fool," the colonel said. He grinned suddenly. "What's more, I told him so. He should have known that I wouldn't abandon you. The man's a nitwitted half-baked idiot."

Tomkin came in with Chris and Steve and the tea tray.

"Paddy Joe looks as if the world's suddenly turned upside down and he can't really make head or tail of it," Chris said, grinning. "It's OK, Kiddo. You're all right now."

"Martha's here too," Tomkin said. "She and I fight like cats, but it does her good. If she hadn't been worried sick about you, Paddy Joe, she'd have perked up no end. I've told her you're here. She was in her room resting."

Martha was already at the door. She had hurried too much she was out of breath, and she embarrassed Paddy Joe by hugging him tight and kissing him and crying all over his cheek.

"Oh, Lambie, Lambie, you had us all worried sick," Martha said, and Paddy Joe felt worse than ever. He had not thought of how they would feel.

Tomkin had made sandwiches and there were crumpets and one of Martha's chocolate cakes. Paddy Joe ate little. He was content to sit quiet, watching everyone else, feeling that he had indeed fallen into safety and the world, that had been so desolate, was already a brighter place. The colonel, who understood boys very well, said very little about his escapades, and the policeman who called in answer to Tomkin's telephone call, was also considerate. Paddy Joe was safe. That was all that mattered, for the moment.

Steve and Chris said goodbye, and went on their way to continue their holiday. Tomkin stocked them up with food from the pantry, and home-made cakes, and apples from the garden, and Paddy Joe, waving to them, hoped that he would see them again.

That night he curled up in his own chair, and the colonel and Tomkin and Martha listened to his adventures, and Storm lay with his head on Paddy Joe's shoe.

"Everything will be, as much as possible, just as it was before," the colonel said, as Paddy Joe was going to bed. "You'll be going back to school, and we'll be here. We need to make some changes. There aren't any stables here for Thunder and Lightning, so we'll have to build some, which will mean altering the garden. I thought that you might like a pony of your own. We'll go and find one as soon as we've sorted everything out.

I've told Mr Throstle you're home," he added.

"He really did say he'd have Storm put to sleep," Paddy Joe said, anxiously.

The colonel nodded.

"He thought he was doing everything for the best, Paddy Joe," he said. "You see, your grandmother never made a will. If she had, she would have made sure that I was your guardian, and that I looked after Storm. We'd talked about it, often. But she hated the thought of leaving you alone and neither Mr Throstle nor I could get her to put everything down on paper. He knew what she wanted, but he felt I was too old to take on a boy and a dog. He seems to have thought that if the dog weren't there, and you were in a Boys' Home, it would be best for all of us. However, I soon put him right about that. And if anything happens to me, my son will look after you. He's promised and you like Dave, don't you?"

Dave, who was in the Navy, was enormous fun. Paddy Joe lay awake in his own room, watching the moonlight on the bare wall. His postcards had all been spoiled by the bad trout, which had marked them, but he could find more pictures to hang up in their places. The colonel had put Storm's bed in the corner of Paddy Joe's room. He could hear the dog breathing. Tomorrow they were going to the vet to make sure there was no further danger from the snake-bite. There was still a hard lump on the dog's shoulder, which was sore to the touch.

Paddy Joe climbed out of bed. Storm followed him, and together they looked out of the window. There was an owl in the apple tree. Light shone on the turning head that seemed able to swivel right round on its body and on the enormous eyes that stared straight at Paddy Joe as if wondering about him. The apple tree smelled of promise. The apples were ripe.

There was a movement under the tree. It was Sam. Paddy Joe ran downstairs. Tomkin was in the kitchen, smoking his pipe, and looking thoughtfully at the fire which needed mending.

"Sam hasn't had his banana," Paddy Joe said.

There was a banana in the pantry. Tomkin peeled it, and they went outside. The rain had ceased, and a warm wind soothed the apple boughs and ruffled Paddy Joe's pyjamas. He knelt at the foot of the tree, comforted by darkness. Sam, smelling his favourite fruit, came eagerly on short legs that moved remarkably swiftly over the grass and took the whole banana, piece by piece, from Paddy Joe's hand. The little mouth was soft against the boy's palm. Storm, interested, came to look, and sniffed at Sam, and licked the tortoise's head. They were old cronies. Sam was in ecstasy. He finished eating and tucked comfortably inside his shell.

Paddy Joe stood in the garden. Tomkin leaned against the apple tree, his eyes on the boy, his grin, loplipped, on his mouth. He was very little taller than Paddy Joe, a neat man, dark-haired, brown skin wrinkled by weather. A train went by. Its lights seemed to flash off and on as it slipped among the trees. The people in it were islanded, safe, going about their own affairs. Twelve days ago Paddy Joe had envied them. Tonight he wouldn't change places with them for a fortune. He watched the train till it was out of sight, and turned to Tomkin.

"We're going to finish our interrupted holiday," Tomkin said. "This time you and Storm are coming, too, Paddy Joe. We're going back to Smuggler's Island, which is where the colonel goes fishing. You wait. The adventures you've had just now will be tame beside those you're going to have."

He ruffled Paddy Joe's hair. Paddy Joe leaned

against the apple trunk in his turn and felt the teasing wind. Storm stood beside him, close against his leg. It was peaceful outside in the garden. A moth danced against the window, a nightjar churred softly, and downwind an owl hooted as it flew.

Paddy Joe smiled into the darkness.

He was home. He was going on holiday. One day, in the far away future, he would be a vet and look after animals, and he would be the best vet in the whole world.

The moon shone full on his face.

"Yiyeeee," yelled Paddy Joe, and Storm jumped at him and a moment later boy and dog were rolling together in a wild romp, impelled by delight, and the week of misery was forgotten.

THE END

DOUBLE TROUBLE! by Joyce Stranger   75p
0 552 52132 9   Carousel

There was a yelp from the last dog, and it stopped searching to lick frenziedly at its paw. The dog was high on the hill and the rocks there were steep and jagged. The handler running to his dog yelled back.

'Glass! He's cut an artery!'

Tim raced towards them. Up over the rocks, panting and gasping for breath, his feet sliding from under him. He was whipping the cord from his anorak as he ran. He would need to tourniquet if he could – if only the cut weren't in the wrong place. The handler was kneeling beside his dog, pressing his hand over the wound. Blood spurted all around him ...

Tim's new life as a vet was full of ups and downs; some were happy, some were sad, some were just infuriating – but at times like these his worries were lost in the desperate struggle to help an animal in need. This was what he was trained for – this was truly where he wanted to be ...

An exciting sequel to VET ON CALL by the same author.

JASON by Joyce Stranger   60p
0 552 52113 2   Carousel

Nobody wanted the pup. He was born to a pedigree golden labrador bitch and his father was a giant mastiff. The owner of the bitch was furious and got rid of Jason as quickly as he could.

His first master didn't really like him very much – he only wanted him as a guard dog, and one day Jason ran away looking, although he did not know it, for a master whom he could love. And when he found Duncan Grant, a boy who was as lonely as Jason, they were bound together in an instant and enduring friendship.

But even then Jason's troubles were not over, for Duncan's father would not let his son keep the dog ...

If you would like to receive a newsletter telling you about our new children's books, fill in the coupon with your name and address and send it to:

Gillian Osband,

Transworld Publishers Ltd,

Century House,

61–63 Uxbridge Road, Ealing,

London, W5 5SA

Name...

Address..

....

CHILDREN'S NEWSLETTER

All the books on the previous pages are available at your bookshop or can be ordered direct from Transworld Publishers Ltd., Cash Sales Dept. P.O. Box 11, Falmouth, Cornwall.

Please send full name and address together with cheque or postal order—no currency, and allow 45p per book to cover postage and packing (plus 20p each for additional copies).